THE
STOLEN
YEARS

GLORIA REPP

Original title:
Dave Durant and the Mystery of the Stone House

Bob Jones University Press, Greenville, South Carolina 29614

The Stolen Years

Edited by Laurie Garner

Cover and illustrations by Cheryl Weikel

©1989 by Bob Jones University Press
Greenville, South Carolina 29614

ISBN 0-89084-481-X

Printed in the United States of America

20   19   18   17   16   15   14   13   12   11   10   9

For Andrew

PUBLISHER'S NOTE

Young David Durant has spent his life in a godly environment and has gone faithfully to Sunday school whenever he could. Last year he even won an ivory-handled pocketknife for memorizing a hundred Bible verses. His personal relationship with God is cool, however, and deep inside, he wonders how practical it is to depend on God's love and leave everything up to Him.

When David and his sister arrive in St. Louis, hoping to find a home with the grandfather they have never met, David is dismayed to feel that he is not welcome. He sets himself to find out why, and God uses His powerful Word and a baffling series of events connected with the family's missing silver pistols to draw David closer to Himself. In David's search for the pistols, he makes friends with a sprightly old French lady and a dark-haired girl who demonstrate God's loving care and convince him of his need for God's direction.

After he asks God to take control of his life, David's trust is tested and deepened as he seeks to conquer his fears, cope with his grandfather's bitterness, and solve the mystery that has divided his family for twenty years.

I will restore to you the years that the locust hath eaten. (Joel 2:25)

Contents

Chapter One
Call the Police!

David put a hand on his sister's small shoulder as they joined the stream of hurrying passengers. Not much longer to wait now, he thought, following the crowd down the long airport corridor. It sure felt good to get off that airplane.

He pulled his sister out of the way as a plump, silver-haired woman pressed past them. "Remember last time—you stepped on her toes," he warned.

Susan shook back her blond hair and threw him a bright, mischievous glance. "I didn't mean to, you know. That lady didn't have to get so mad." She glanced at the crowd of people in front of them. "Why is everybody walking so fast? Where are they going?"

"I guess they're all going to pick up their luggage like we are," he answered. "Then we'll wait for our grandfather."

The words sounded reassuring, and he wanted to say them again. *Our grandfather*. It didn't matter that David had never met the man. It only mattered that he was their dad's father, and now they were going to have a home with him.

David tried to ignore his anxiety. The letter had said that they were to come. That meant everything would be all right. Didn't it?

They stopped at a clattering baggage carousel to look for their suitcases. In front of them stood a blond boy and the silver-haired woman. As David bent to put down his flight bag, an impatient passenger who was shouldering his way through the crowd sent him stumbling into the woman.

She turned and snapped at him, "What's the matter with you kids? Can't you stand on your own two feet?"

David tried to explain. "I'm sorry, but someone pushed me."

She paid no attention to his apology, angrily patting her silver curls into place as she moved away. Suddenly she grabbed at her wrist. "My watch—it's gone!" Her voice rose. "My bracelet too—I've been robbed! Call the police!"

Instinctively David stepped backward. Everyone else was backing away from her too.

She spun around and glared at him. "You!" she cried. "You took them, didn't you? You ran into me on purpose. I know how you kids operate. You tried it back there on the airplane, too. Why hasn't somebody called the police?"

David could only stare at her in astonishment. A gray-haired policeman emerged from a doorway, looked the crowd over, and spoke soothingly to the woman. "Is there a problem, ma'am?" The deep voice sounded patient and resigned.

Excitedly the woman waved at David and repeated her accusation.

While she was talking, David saw his sister scowling back at her. Before Susan could speak up and make everything worse, he leaned down, whispering, "Don't worry—she's all mixed up. We didn't touch anything of hers."

The policeman looked from the older woman to David. "You're making a complaint against this young man?" he asked.

"I certainly am. Why, he almost knocked me over, and then my jewelry was gone." The woman lifted her chin. "He can't be allowed to get away with it."

David shook his head in protest and the policeman gave him a sharp glance. "Did anybody else see what happened?"

No one in the waiting crowd moved or spoke.

David searched for the blond boy who had been standing next to the woman. That kid would have seen the whole thing. But he had disappeared.

The policeman eyed David now, examining him, and he felt a prickle of fear. "Are you two traveling alone?"

David nodded.

"How about coming with me for a minute?" It was a command, though, not a request. The policeman turned back to the woman. "Ma'am, would you please wait here?"

Silently David picked up his flight bag and grabbed for Susan's hand. They followed the policeman down the hall and into a small office crowded with radio equipment, three chairs, and a battered desk.

After closing the door, the policeman sat down at the desk and picked up a sheet of paper. "Let's see what you have in your pockets," he said quietly.

From his shirt pocket David slowly pulled a folder of airline tickets and the letter. Then he emptied the rest of his pockets while Susan huddled on a gray metal chair.

The policeman began writing. "What's your name? Your sister's name?"

David tried to smooth the nervous jiggle out of his voice as he gave their names.

"How old are you? Where'd you come from? Where are you going?"

"I'm sixteen—my sister's eight," David answered. "We came from New Jersey. We lived there with my aunt, and we're on our way to our grandfather's house, here in St. Louis."

"What's your aunt's name and address?"

"Lucy Morgan. She died." David shifted his gaze to the narrow white stripe on the man's blue pants so that his eyes wouldn't give away the emptiness inside him.

But the policeman didn't look up. "Your grandfather's name and phone number?"

"His name is Philip Durant. I wrote his phone number on that envelope." David waved at the letter he had taken out of his shirt pocket.

The man gave him a quick, interested glance. "So you're Philip Durant's grandson?" He scribbled down the number. "All right, David, you can put your stuff away. Now, what happened out there?"

While David explained, the policeman unzipped the flight bag, sorted through it, and then checked Susan's pockets. Straightening up, he said, "Well, it looks like the lady made a mistake, doesn't it?" His face lost its stern expression. "We've had a couple pieces of jewelry stolen around here lately, and everybody's getting nervous. How long are you going to stay at your grandfather's?"

"We've come to live with him." For Susan's sake, David made his answer confident.

The man nodded. "All right, you're free to go. Just be sure we can find you if we need any more information."

The silver-haired woman still waited in the corridor. "Well?" she demanded.

"Please step in here, ma'am," the policeman said in his polite voice.

Relief swept over David as the door shut behind her. "Come on, Susan, let's get our suitcases." He headed back down the hall toward the baggage carousel. Was their grandfather already there, waiting for them?

He stopped and faced his sister. "Hey, we'd better not tell anybody what just happened, okay?" He fumbled for the words he needed to convince her. "We don't know our grandfather very well, and this might not look too good, even though it wasn't my fault."

"Sure," Susan agreed. "I just want to forget about it anyway." She threw an outraged glance over her shoulder. "Mean old thing!"

He nodded, but he was wondering why the policeman had asked for Grandfather's phone number. Was he going to phone and tell Grandfather what had happened?

By the time they reached the baggage pickup area, most of the crowd had come and gone. David made a quick survey of the bustling airport concourse. Nope, no one seemed to be waiting for them.

Slowly he took the blue baggage stubs from the ticket folder in his shirt pocket. When he put the folder back, his fingers brushed the envelope beside it—the heavy, cream-colored envelope that still smelled faintly of lavender. Without even opening it, he could picture the dark, angular strokes of the handwriting on the letter inside.

It was the letter he had found in Aunt Lucy's desk, just as she had said he would, on that last night.

He glanced down at his blond little sister standing beside him, watching the suitcases on their merry-go-round. He hadn't told Susan how uncertain he'd felt about this trip. She'd been so happy at the prospect of visiting the grandfather they'd never seen.

But the letter hadn't come from him. In fact, David wasn't sure who it was from.

David hadn't told Susan that, either. She'd had plenty of upsetting things to face this past week, with Aunt Lucy's funeral and all the confusion. It would be hard enough on her until Dad came back and they could really settle down in a home of their own. How soon would that be? Just thinking about it made him feel a sudden burst of longing.

"There's my blue suitcase," Susan exclaimed, pointing. "And there's the green one. Oh, quick, David, get them!"

As he reached for the suitcases, he caught sight of a tall, broad-shouldered man striding toward them through the crowd. Could this be their grandfather?

Chapter Two
Who Is Aunt Jeanne?

The man's face creased into a good-natured smile as he pushed past another traveler to greet them. "Well, you must be David and Susan," he said in a hearty voice. "I'm Bob Jonson, a friend of your grandfather's. Had to come down here to pick up something for the airplane, so I told him I might as well bring you two back with me."

It wasn't Grandfather after all.

David felt oddly relieved as he shook the big, work-hardened hand. Beside him, Susan was smiling her sunny smile that meant she liked the man, and Mr. Jonson, bending low to talk to her, was obviously charmed. But that was typical of Susan, David reminded himself. His sister liked just about everyone, and she made friends effortlessly. He'd often wished that he had her sociable nature.

Mr. Jonson picked up their suitcases and bulldozed his way through the crowded airport to the parking lot. Susan and David hurried to keep up with him. After they had loaded all the suitcases into a faded blue pickup truck, Susan climbed in to sit next to Mr. Jonson. She chattered about their trip as they joined the rush of cars thronging the expressway.

From his window seat, David eyed the modern factories, stores, and motels that lined the road. St. Louis sure was different from Cedar Beach, the small town in New Jersey where they had lived with Aunt Lucy.

He turned his thoughts from Cedar Beach. He wanted to forget the dull ache of the past week, particularly that last day with its cold, streaming rain and its sadness—the day of Aunt Lucy's funeral. He was in St. Louis now, and at least it wasn't raining.

In fact, it seemed downright hot for June. He leaned forward to unstick the back of his shirt from the plastic seat covers while he listened to Mr. Jonson telling about his work as an aircraft mechanic. Finally they turned off the expressway onto a wide road that rushed past shopping centers and fast-food restaurants. He sniffed at the unmistakable aroma of French fries. Even though they had eaten on the airplane, he was hungry again.

The sun was setting in a sullen red haze, and he glanced at it to check their direction. Yes, they were still going north. Now the landscape had changed to green fields alternating with clusters of sleek suburban homes. David smothered a yawn and studied the dark clouds massing on the horizon. He had just decided that they were cumulonimbus clouds when a question from Susan caught his attention.

"What's her name?" Susan was asking.

"Jeanne," said Mr. Jonson. "Jeanne LaTour. She's your relative too. Let's see now, she would be your grandfather's cousin, so you'd call her Aunt Jeanne."

"She's a marvelous cook," he went on after a pause. "And it's a good thing she's there or your grandfather would have starved long ago. Once he gets to painting, he just loses track of time."

Wide awake, David listened eagerly to the conversation about his grandfather.

He could still remember the day—years ago—that he had been playing in the attic and had found a painting of a paddle-wheel ferry. After that he had spent many hours staring at it in fascination. He'd managed to find out that his grandfather was the artist who had painted the red ferry boat, but none of the grown-ups seemed willing to answer any more questions, so after a while he had stopped asking. As he grew up, though, he'd dreamed of someday meeting that mysterious painter.

Mr. Jonson laughed. "He's a great guy, your grandfather, and a good pilot too. Well, looks like we're almost there."

They were turning onto a gravel driveway that climbed a steep hill and disappeared into a clump of trees. Now David could see the house—cream-colored, with tall pillars that gleamed pale in the twilight. It was a bigger house than he had expected; grander than he wanted it to be.

"Oh, it's a pretty house!" Susan exclaimed in delight. "And look, it has a crown on top."

Mr. Jonson chuckled. "That's called a widow's walk, Susan. It's sort of a lookout platform on the roof. And you're right: the railing around it does make it look like a crown."

But David couldn't help thinking that the square old house looked silent and withdrawn. Perhaps he had been foolish to hope that welcoming lights would be shining through its windows—that someone would be waiting eagerly to greet them. This house was dark, except for one dimly lit window.

Mr. Jonson braked to a stop in front of the pillared porch and swung out of the truck.

"I'll just drop you kids off here," he said, handing the suitcases down to David. "Go ahead and knock on the door. Looks like your grandfather's up there painting again, but I'm sure Jeanne's in the back somewhere. I'm coming over tomorrow, so I'll see you then." He jumped into the truck, gave them a wave, and was gone before David could thank him.

As the truck rattled off, Susan turned her gaze back to the house. "Look, there's another porch up there and some more posts that go right up to the roof."

David took his time answering. "Yes, that's the balcony, and it's all those pillars that make the house look so tall."

What kind of a man would live in a house like this? His fingers slid across the pocket of his shirt, where the letter crinkled faintly, encouraging him.

Susan giggled, and he could tell that she was nervous. "This porch is big enough for Mr. Jonson to park his truck on," she said, echoing David's thoughts as he looked around the broad space enclosed by white pillars. "Why don't you knock on the door?"

David tried to delay the moment when he had to approach that massive wooden door. "I was going to let you ring the doorbell."

Susan edged closer to the door. She had just reached it when it swung open.

"Well, here you are at last," a soft voice said. "Come into the kitchen." A dark-haired woman motioned them into a long hall that stretched, cool and dim, toward a lighted doorway. Following her, they walked past a curving staircase and two closed doors into a cheerful-looking kitchen.

The woman turned with a swish of her full blue skirt and leaned down to hug Susan. "I am your Aunt Jeanne," she said, and David caught a glimpse of rosy cheeks and warm brown eyes. He brushed the hair off his forehead as she straightened up to greet him.

But then the woman's smile crumpled. She was staring at him, her face white and her eyes wide. In the next instant her face tightened into a polite mask as she murmured something and swung away to take dishes from a cupboard.

David stood there with his own smile stiffening on his face. What had gone wrong?

His aunt took a deep breath, as if to collect herself. Then she turned to Susan, saying a little too brightly, "Would you like a snack, or would you rather just go right up to your rooms?"

The kitchen suddenly felt hot to David. "We're not hungry," he said, giving Susan's shoulder a warning touch. "I think my sister is tired out."

Aunt Jeanne nodded and led them out of the kitchen. As she turned, he caught a whiff of old-fashioned perfume. But it wasn't lavender, like the scent in the letter. No, it was more like . . . violets. He saw that the dark hair gathered smoothly at the nape of her neck was streaked with gray— she was older than he'd thought at first—and now her brown eyes wore a haunted look.

Had he caused that? David wondered. What was the matter with her? And where was Grandfather? As he picked up a suitcase, questions circled inside his head, buzzing like pesky beach flies.

Silently he climbed the creaking staircase behind Susan and his aunt. They were talking in a quiet undertone. Even Susan must have felt subdued in the gloom of this somber house, for she was whispering as she asked her questions.

At the top of the steps, Aunt Jeanne gestured toward a closed door on their right. "Your grandfather's bedroom and studio," she explained. She turned to the left and walked into a broad room furnished with an old-fashioned bed and chest of drawers. "This is Susan's bedroom." Opening a connecting door to a similar room, she added, "And this is yours."

She did not look at David as she spoke, and he noticed that she had not said his name. She waved her hand toward the far end of the bedroom. "There's another little room back there too. You may use it for anything you want." With a hurried pat for Susan, she left them by themselves.

After David had carried up the rest of their suitcases, he decided that he'd better get Susan to bed. He listened more patiently than usual to her sleepy comments while he helped her unpack a few things. Yes, he agreed, Grandfather must be busy painting—that's what artists are like—and they would surely see him tomorrow. Before he left, he pulled back the covers of the big four-poster bed and gave her a good-night hug.

At last he could step into his room, shut the door, and be alone. But even so, he felt uneasy. He found his pajamas and put them on, still thinking about the distress he had seen on Aunt Jeanne's face. What had happened when she looked at him? He didn't think he looked especially strange: dark brown hair, dark eyes, a pretty decent tan. He shook his head, perplexed. And this stuffy room made it hard to concentrate on anything.

One of the old windows yielded reluctantly to his impatient shove, and he leaned out to gulp deep breaths of the warm, pine-scented night. All he could see was the dark outline of pine trees blurred against a black sky. Humidity hung in the air, sticky as black syrup, and he couldn't help thinking about the cool breezes at Cedar Beach.

Maybe we shouldn't have come. He tried to resist the thought, but it only reminded him of the worry that had shadowed Aunt Lucy's face the last time he'd visited her in the hospital.

"I hope I did the right thing, David," she had whispered. "I thought you should know about your grandfather." Then she'd told him of the letter she had written to Missouri only a few weeks before. The reply that had come was in her desk waiting for him—the lavender-scented letter he now carried in his pocket.

Finally Aunt Lucy had closed her eyes and murmured, "Be a peacemaker, David."

He gripped the worn wood of the windowsill. What had she meant about being a peacemaker? He still didn't know.

From the hall, a clock chimed softly, probably the grandfather clock he had seen at the head of the stairs. Grandfather! Tomorrow he'd meet him at last. He couldn't wait— but he was worried about it too. Why hadn't their grandfather come down to greet them tonight? Had the policeman phoned to caution him that his grandson had been accused of stealing something at the airport?

Wearily David left the window and crawled into the wide old bed. A faint scent of violets clung to the smooth sheets, as if Aunt Jeanne still hovered nearby. Resolving not to think about her, he concentrated on naming every star and planet he could remember studying in school.

The next thing he knew, Susan was jiggling his bed, and the room was filled with morning light.

"David!" she exclaimed.

He groaned and burrowed under his pillow.

"Do you know what? I've got a fireplace in my room, and so do you, and my own rocking chair. What's in here?" The bed stopped moving and her voice faded. "Why, it's the neatest little room. You can use it for all your stuff, like a real scientist."

Then she was back beside him. "Come on, get up, this is the most interesting house I've ever been in, and oh! I'm so hungry, aren't you?"

"I sure am," he said, sitting up. "You'd better get out of here and get dressed so we can go down to breakfast."

"I'm going to beat you," she cried, already on her way through the door.

Chapter Three
Meeting 55 Charlie

David hurried to find some clean clothes. He was combing his hair in front of the oval mirror when Susan knocked on his door. "You've got to make your bed and pick up your stuff," he called.

Confident that she would be busy for a few more minutes, he stopped to investigate the small back room. Its walls were lined with empty shelves, and a red braided rug brightened the floor. With a chair and table, it would be a good place to study, just as Susan had said.

His sister burst into the room as he was walking across the rug to look out the window. "What's that orange flag thing above the trees?" she asked.

"That's a windsock," David answered. "You usually see one at an airport. It tells a pilot which way the wind is blowing."

He watched the bright cone of the windsock swivel in the breeze. Mr. Jonson had said that Grandfather was a good pilot. Did he have an airstrip over in that field?

Susan tugged at his shirt. "C'mon, let's go. I can smell breakfast." He followed her down the stairs, listening anxiously for voices, wondering if his grandfather would be there.

In a room adjoining the kitchen, they found Aunt Jeanne arranging glasses of orange juice on a long table that was set near wide windows. The dining room's faded green wallpaper still had a silky sheen that lightened the dark furniture. Above the table hung a small, glittering chandelier, and Susan eyed it with pleasure.

Aunt Jeanne turned quickly to greet them. "Susan!" she exclaimed as the little girl ran to hug her. "Did you sleep well?"

"Yes I did—it's such a nice big bed and where is Grandfather?" Susan answered all in one breath.

"He's coming down the steps now. Let's go see him." She cast a smile in David's direction without really looking at him, and took Susan with her to the door. He wanted to follow, but an inner caution held him back.

The man entering the room looked just as David had imagined—tall and keen-eyed, with graying black hair and a clipped gray moustache. He leaned down to put an arm around Susan, who smiled back at him, and Aunt Jeanne murmured, "Bonjour, Philippe," adding something else in rapid French. David watched them, feeling as if he had been left outside and was peering in through a window.

Grandfather turned to David, and the smile he'd had for Susan faded. His black eyebrows lifted a fraction of an inch, and some swift emotion flared in his dark eyes, then was gone.

"And this is Dave," Aunt Jeanne said unnecessarily in the awkward pause. "Now let's sit down and eat. The eggs—" She hurried into the kitchen.

Now his grandfather spoke to him. The voice was polite but cold. The words were not what he longed to hear. "How are you, Dave? Did you two have a good trip? Let's see now, Susan, you sit over here, and we'll be all ready. Here come the eggs."

Aunt Jeanne put the platter of scrambled eggs down in front of Grandfather, who served Susan and then passed them to David. He helped himself blindly and handed the dish to Aunt Jeanne. At least Susan was talking—giving a detailed account of the airplane trip—and no one seemed to be watching him.

David sat with his eyes fixed on the small yellow mound of eggs before him, trying to hide his dismay. One French expression that Aunt Jeanne had used—*Prends garde*—caught like a burr and hung in his mind, prickling uncomfortably. *Take care,* she'd said, as if she were warning Grandfather about him. But why?

"Would you like some toast?" Aunt Jeanne's soft voice still had the faint music of a French accent. When he met her gaze, she glanced away quickly.

The homemade toast was thick and crunchy, but even while he was telling himself how good it tasted, questions churned inside. Why couldn't she stand to look at him? Why had his grandfather looked so surprised, just now?

The drone of an approaching airplane reached them through the open window, and even Susan stopped talking to listen.

"That will be Bob Jonson," Grandfather said, taking another piece of toast. "He's here to help us finish up 55 Charlie."

He smiled at the question on Susan's face. "You don't know about 55 Charlie, do you? Well, eat up your breakfast, and we'll go down to see him. You can meet Bruce too."

David followed his grandfather and Susan down a dirt path to the clump of trees where they had seen the windsock. Mr. Jonson must have landed his small plane in the long pasture, for it was already parked by a weather-beaten brown barn.

"This is our hangar," Grandfather said as they reached the barn. He led Susan to a blue airplane parked just inside the wide doors. "And here is 55 Charlie."

David felt himself tighten inside. He hadn't been near a small plane like this for almost seven years—wasn't that long enough to forget? Taking a deep breath, he ignored the fear, hoping it would go away. He licked the dry taste off his lips and studied the short, dark-haired boy who was working on the propeller. He was probably a couple of years older than David, judging from his wispy moustache and long black sideburns.

"What a cute little airplane!" Susan was saying. "Is it yours?"

"Yes, it's mine and Mr. Jonson's," Grandfather answered. "It was in pretty bad shape when we bought it, and we're fixing it up, with Bruce's help."

"Hi, kids. This is Bruce, my son," Mr. Jonson said heartily. "We've almost got this prop back on, Philip." He turned to Bruce. "Hand me the three-quarter-inch open-end, will you?"

As Bruce picked up the wrench, he gave David a quick glance, his gray eyes wary. He didn't say anything, perhaps because Susan was already asking about the plane.

"What happened to it? The paint is chipped, and look at this wing." She pointed to the bare metal tip on one of the blue wings.

"It was blown over in a windstorm one night when the tie-down ropes came loose," answered Grandfather in his deep voice. "That damaged a wing and bent the prop, so after we bought it, we replaced this wing tip. We just got the prop back from the repair shop. It won't be long before 55 Charlie is ready to fly again."

He gave the plane a pat and walked around to its tail. "Bruce, did you work on rigging the rudder yet?"

"Nope, but that's the last thing," Bruce said. "Dad says we can run it up tomorrow."

"Bruce is our right-hand man," Grandfather explained to Susan and David. "He practically grew up at that airport where his dad works, and he's got his pilot's license already."

He gave Bruce a warm smile, and David wished the smile were for him.

Mr. Jonson broke in. "Yes, sir! And to listen to Bruce, you'd think he knows as much about fixing airplanes as all the rest of us put together."

Everyone laughed, Mr. Jonson loudest of all. But David saw the slow flush creeping up Bruce's neck and wondered how the boy felt about his father's teasing.

"Mr. Jonson, your airplane is awfully pretty," Susan said, eyeing the sleek, bronze-striped little plane parked next to the hangar. She cocked her head. "How come it doesn't have any door?"

"When we use it for skydivers, we take off the door on that side so it's easier for them to jump out," he said with a smile. "If you look inside, you'll see that there's no back seat or copilot's seat, either. That's so we can fit in more skydivers. Their parachutes take up a lot of space."

She gave him an interested glance. "Do you jump out of the plane too?"

Mr. Jonson chuckled. "No, I'm the pilot. I fly the plane for the skydivers' club. Your grandfather does too, when he isn't busy painting."

To Bruce he said, "Let's go look at that rudder." Then he motioned to David's grandfather. "Philip, I want to show you something back here."

While the men bent over the tail of the airplane, Susan was busy reading the numbers on its side. "David, what does this mean: N1755C?"

"That's the registration number for the airplane," he answered. "Sort of its own special name."

"Why do they call it Charlie, anyway?"

David was conscious of Bruce listening, and he was glad he knew the answer. "Usually an airplane number ends with a letter of the alphabet, and it would be easy to confuse the ones like *S* and *F* when a pilot is talking on the radio. So each letter has a certain word that makes it easy to understand. The word for *C* is *Charlie*."

"Oh, I get it," Susan said. She glanced over at the bronze-striped plane. "Mr. Jonson's plane has an *S* on it. What's that for?"

"Sierra."

"What's that?"

"Well, it a range of mountains, and—"

"Oh, never mind," she interrupted. "What I'd really like to do is see where that path over there goes." She darted to her grandfather's side. "I'm going to explore. Is that all right?"

He looked down at her and smiled. "That's fine. Just don't fall into the river." He spoke to David without actually looking at him. "You'd better go along with her until she gets used to this area."

"Sure." Anything to get away from here, he thought, hiding his relief. He left the hangar and joined Susan.

Chapter Four
Are You French?

The trail past the hangar narrowed as it led them into dense woods, and trees crowded close with branches that arched overhead to shut out the sky. "Oh, David!" Susan exclaimed, skipping along beside him. "Isn't it nice in these woods? It smells so good, and the trees are all sort of soft and friendly-looking."

He grinned at her. "Sure is a change from the beach in New Jersey."

New Jersey . . . he shouldn't have reminded her. Aunt Lucy wasn't there to go back to anymore. During all the years that they'd been separated from Dad, at least they'd always had Aunt Lucy. He glanced at his sister anxiously, but she was walking with her blond head tilted back, watching the birds flash and twitter through the trees.

Maybe it doesn't bother her as much as it does me, he thought. He hated not having a real family of his own. It seemed that he was always wondering what was going to happen to them next.

Susan dashed ahead of him. "I think the river must be near. Maybe it's just over this hill." She ran up a slope and stopped short, exclaiming, "Oh, look—here it is!"

Following close behind, David stopped too. He caught his breath at the sight of the gray-green expanse of rippling water that swept below them. He'd never seen a river so wide and powerful. As they stood in a shared silence of delight, something in him answered to its mighty surge, its restless gallop past the steep bluff.

Slowly the shining moment faded. This river was different from the ocean, he thought. When they'd lived near the ocean, he could stand and look across the glittering blue all the way to the horizon and say, "Dad is right over there; he's just on the other side of that water." But now they were hundreds of miles from the ocean. Besides—David had to keep reminding himself—Dad was in England now, in the hospital. He wasn't even on the mission field anymore.

The last time David had seen his father was five years ago. Even then Dad's face had been thin and pale from sickness. David picked up a handful of stones and flung them into the river, one by one. Dad was supposed to have been reassigned permanently to the States. They had planned so happily to be all together again, to live with Aunt Lucy. Then she had died, and Dad had gotten too sick to travel, and here they were, stuck with relatives who—

"Come on, let's go this way," Susan urged. He hurled the last stone as far as he could and walked after her, around the bend of the river.

"Look, there's a girl down there." Susan stopped and peered over the edge of the bluff. "She's—"

"Shhh!" David hissed. That was all he needed—for Susan to find some girl; then he'd have to listen to them giggle all the way along the river trail.

Susan pointed down to an immense pile of rocks that jutted out into the river. At the far end of the embankment sat a slender girl, probably about David's own age. The sun glinted on her smooth black hair as she bent over a pad of drawing paper.

"Isn't she pretty? How did she get down there?" Susan said. "Let's go—"

"No," David said firmly, "I don't think she wants to be disturbed." He turned his sister around on the path.

"You never let me have any fun," she protested.

"Aunt Jeanne said something about an early lunch," he reminded her. "You don't want to miss that, do you?"

"Well, okay." The prospect of food seemed to change Susan's mind, as he knew it would.

"Aunt Jeanne is nice, don't you think?" she said, trotting to keep up with his long strides. "I like her. Did you hear her talking to Grandfather in another language?"

"Yes, that was French," David answered. He had picked up a lot of French when his parents were at language school in France, but now he was hoping that Susan wouldn't ask if he'd understood what Aunt Jeanne had said.

"Oh, French," said Susan. "I forgot that you know some too. Well, I wonder where she learned to talk it so fast."

"Why don't you ask her, Miss Curiosity?" He was used to Susan's lively interest in everyone they met, but he couldn't resist teasing her about it. Besides, he'd like to find out some more about Aunt Jeanne too.

After lunch, when Grandfather had gone upstairs to paint, Susan took the chance to talk to their aunt.

"Are you French, Aunt Jeanne?" she began.

"Yes, I am," her aunt said warmly. "And so are you."

"I am?"

"Certainly. Come with me. I will show you something very interesting." Aunt Jeanne led them across the hall to a long room filled with books and paintings.

"This is our library," she said. "You are welcome to read any of these books."

It would be a good place to read, David thought. He pictured himself curled up in one of those worn leather chairs, in front of that big fireplace on a chilly day. Maybe that's what Dad had done when he was a boy.

He paused beside a painting of a misty river that looked like rippling silver. "Did my grandfather paint this?"

"Yes," said Aunt Jeanne, and he could hear the pride in her voice. "These others are his too."

David gazed in admiration at the paintings of riverboats and river wildlife. Now he had finally met the artist he'd wondered about for so many years. But the man was cold and remote—still a stranger. And the worst part was not knowing why.

Aunt Jeanne crossed the room to a long sheet of paper pinned beside the bookshelves. "This is what I wanted to show you. See, here is our family tree. I've been working on it for months."

She pointed to a name at the top of a complex pyramid of names and dates connected by lines. "Here is the first Philippe of the family, born in France in 1597." Her slim finger traced the lines down through several generations of names. "Now here is a Philippe who lived during the French Revolution. He escaped death by coming to America, and his son, David, was born in St. Louis in 1820."

"Just like your name, David," said Susan. "But why is it called a tree, Aunt Jeanne?"

"Because it shows all the branches of the family." Her aunt pointed to the left side of the paper. "See, this is the part of the family that stayed in France when Philippe fled to America. That was my branch of the family. I was born in France and grew up there."

"Well now, let's see," she went on, "here's your great-grandfather, William. He was born in this very house; then, of course, your grandfather was born here too."

"Where's my name?" asked Susan.

"I'll put that on now," Aunt Jeanne said hastily. "You and your brother will fit in right here under your father's name." She unpinned the paper from the wall and sat down at a round table to add their names in delicate script. As David watched, he remembered the letter he'd carried in his pocket yesterday. He still didn't know who had written it. Could it have been her?

As soon as he and Susan went back to their rooms to finish unpacking, he pulled out the cream-colored envelope and studied the letter again. The sharply angled script could never be mistaken for Aunt Jeanne's lacy writing, and he already knew that it wasn't from Grandfather, because the writer referred to him in the letter. Who would have signed it with only a quickly sketched daisy?

Susan appeared in the doorway with a book, and David slid the letter into the top drawer of his chest. "I'm finished," she said. "Want to read?"

"Well, I'm not nearly done, but I can listen to you." Susan's teacher had told her to be sure to practice reading this summer. Most of the time David didn't mind listening to her, since he liked reading so much himself.

"You have a pretty quilt on your bed, just like mine," Susan observed, settling herself against his pillows. She opened the book. "This is a story about a teddy bear who got left in somebody's attic."

While she read, David unlocked the suitcase that held the beginnings of his insect collection. The top of the bureau would be a good place to keep his stuff: a couple of collecting jars, five small white boxes of insect specimens, and a few empty pillboxes. His identification books could go there too. He'd hang the butterfly net on the hook behind the door and hope that Aunt Jeanne wouldn't be squeamish about having insects in the room. Although he'd collected several common specimens in New Jersey, he was counting on making some interesting additions now that he was here in Missouri.

It was all because of Mr. Taylor. David smiled, remembering. His high school science teacher had called him in during the last week of school. "Make sure you don't get lazy over the summer, David," he'd said in his abrupt manner. "You've done good work for me this year. Now I want you to plan a project and stick to it. How about entomology? You might like studying insects for a change."

Without waiting for an answer, Mr. Taylor had continued. "You can come over and tell me your plans in a few days. And I'll expect a complete report in September."

It wouldn't make any difference to Mr. Taylor that David might not return to that school in the fall. He always said that he believed in encouraging his students who showed scientific potential. David had heard that several of Mr. Taylor's former students were respected scientists now, and they still wrote him letters about their work. Yes, he'd be waiting for that report in September, no matter what.

David sighed. Maybe it would be good to have a project under way, to take his mind off the situation here. He pushed one of the small pillboxes into his pocket. That was something else he'd learned from Mr. Taylor: always carry a pillbox along in case an interesting specimen turned up.

By now Susan had gone back to her room, and she was so quiet in there that she must have fallen asleep. This would be a good time to explore, perhaps down by the river. He wanted to make a map of the area and find a stick for his butterfly net. This morning he'd been so busy listening to Susan that he hadn't had much of a chance to observe anything.

When he reached the river, he scrambled down the steep bank to a narrow border of sand and walked upstream beside the swiftly flowing water until the skeleton of a fallen tree barred his way. After a quick survey of its bare limbs, he snapped off a branch that was long enough to serve as a handle for his net. He could strip away the bark and smooth out the knobby spots later, in his room.

When he climbed back up the sandy bank, he dislodged a small wiggling creature from its hiding place. It slid past him, and he picked it up to examine critically: two legs per segment and lots of segments. It must be a millipede; not really an insect, but he'd keep it anyway.

As he dropped it into his pillbox, thunder grumbled in the distance. He glanced quickly at the clouds scudding overhead and decided that he'd run out of time to hunt for more specimens. Hurrying now, he soon reached the woods, and in the fading light everything looked more dim and shadowy than he had remembered.

He rounded a bend in the trail and saw a lean, dark-jacketed figure striding through the trees ahead of him. It turned off to the right, giving him a glimpse of pale-colored hair, then melted into the gloom and was gone.

Chapter Five
Unexpected Company

"That looked like a guy carrying something," David muttered to himself, peering through the dusk. "Couldn't have been Bruce—he was too tall. Where'd he disappear to, anyway?"

Before long he reached a faint path branching off to the right of the main trail. He was tempted to explore it, but he changed his mind when a gust of wind shook the leaves above him. Raindrops pattered lightly all around, and he headed toward the house instead.

Beside the back porch stood a huge stump, burned to a hollow, blackened shell. He paused to glance curiously into it, thinking that it must have been one of the big old pine trees that surrounded the house. Maybe it had been struck by lightning. That would've made quite a bonfire.

As he bounded onto the porch, David was greeted by the aroma of roasting meat. Smelled like a good supper. He ran up the stairs two at a time to put his stick away and wash his grimy hands.

In the dining room he found Susan and Aunt Jeanne standing at the entrance to the small side porch. "Watching for the storm?" he asked, crossing the room to join them.

Aunt Jeanne eyed the dark, billowing clouds massed above the trees. "I do not like storms," she said with a shudder, and turned away into the kitchen.

As they began to eat, David could hear thunder rumbling closer. A chilly breeze swept through the screened door of the porch, filling the room with the fresh, sharp scent of rain. Aunt Jeanne poked at her food and twisted her napkin into a knot. Grandfather had not appeared for supper, and no one seemed to have very much to say. Even Susan was quiet, although she ate her way steadily through a thick slice of roast beef.

Mr. Jonson was right about Aunt Jeanne's being a good cook, David thought, helping himself to more meat and scalloped potatoes. He was reaching for the salad when lightning flared and a deafening crack of thunder shattered the silence. Wind, gusting wildly, tore through the pine trees, and he jumped up to shut the wooden porch door. As he locked it, rain slashed across the windows of the dining room.

Lightning flashed again and again, and Aunt Jeanne's fork clattered to her plate. She clapped her hands to her ears, cringing in the strange, greenish light, while thunder rolled over their heads.

As the thunder died away, David heard quick footsteps on the stairs. His grandfather hurried into the room, and Aunt Jeanne sprang to her feet. She clutched at him in silent terror, and he put an arm around her, speaking soothingly in French as he led her across the hall to the library.

Susan slid her chair closer to David. "Poor Aunt Jeanne," she murmured while the storm roared around the house. "She told me that she doesn't know why she's so scared of storms like this—she never used to be."

His sister sent him a curious glance and added, "Maybe it would help if you told her, like you keep telling me, that it's just because of too much satic 'lectricity in the clouds."

"Static electricity," he corrected her. " But I don't think that knowing the scientific facts will help Aunt Jeanne," he added, half to himself. "It sounds to me as if she's got an irrational fear."

"What's that?"

"Like you said, she's scared but she doesn't know why. C'mon, let's clear away these dishes for her."

Later that evening, while David was stripping the bark off the stick he'd brought home from the river, he thought about Aunt Jeanne's fear of storms. He'd never seen a grownup so afraid. And Grandfather must have known how she felt, because he got there right away. He'd been nice to her, too.

Slowly David sliced a long strip of gray bark from the stick. The more he thought about it, the more it seemed that his grandfather always had a smile for Susan, but not for him. Had Grandfather found out what had happened at the airport? Was that why he looked at David with such a cold expression? It didn't make sense. There had to be something else.

He closed the blade on his knife and set it carefully on the bureau, admiring its ivory handle. He sure had worked hard to earn it. He'd had to memorize a hundred Bible verses, just to win that contest in Sunday school. David ran his fingers over the verse engraved on the knife's handle: *Call unto me.* What did those words mean? He never felt like calling to God—and besides, He didn't seem to be very real, not anymore.

A memory flashed into his mind, a picture of the radiance on Aunt Lucy's face when she had talked about going to be with the Lord. God had been real enough to her. And sometimes, back when he'd been sitting in church with the other kids, God had felt real to him too. But not here, not now.

He bent down to pick up the scraps of bark, and a sudden scrabbling below the window jerked him upright. As he turned toward the sound, a large smoke-colored cat bounded onto the windowsill. She leaped to his bed and padded across it, leaving wet paw prints on the quilt. Beside his pillow, she paused, studying him with glowing yellow eyes.

"Well, where did you come from?" David asked, delighted. The cat blinked at him and settled down, licking the rain from her fluffy gray tail. "You must be a Persian," he said, leaning over to stroke her long, silky fur. Gently he rubbed the white patch under her chin and was rewarded by a deep rumbling purr.

Later on, when he got into bed, the cat curled up near his feet as if she belonged there. The weight of her body was a comforting warmth against him, and her unexplained presence provided a welcome diversion for his thoughts. "Maybe tomorrow I can find out where you live," he murmured, and then he fell asleep.

When he awoke the next morning, David looked first for the cat, but she was gone. Disappointed, he leaned out the window. Below him stretched the roof of the small porch that adjoined the dining room. He could almost reach down and touch the curling tendrils of a woody, purple-flowered vine that twisted up the pillars.

"What are you looking at?" asked Susan from the doorway.

"I'm just checking out the escape route for my cat," he answered.

"Your cat?"

After David told her about the gray Persian, Susan had to lean out the window too. "Imagine that cat climbing right up the vine! I wish I'd been here. But maybe she'll come back." She turned from the window, adding, "Hey, remember what happens today?"

"What?"

"You know, the test flight for 55 Charlie. Remember what Mr. Jonson said?"

"That's right," David answered, trying to match her enthusiasm.

At the breakfast table, he was glad Susan joined in the general spirit of anticipation so that all he had to do was listen. She talked excitedly about the test flight with Grandfather, who seemed anxious to get breakfast finished. Even Aunt Jeanne walked down with them to watch the test flight.

When they reached the hangar, Mr. Jonson's blue pickup truck was already parked outside. The blue airplane had been pulled out of the hangar, and he and Bruce were doing something to its engine. Standing beside them was a tall blond boy wearing sunglasses, about Bruce's age.

Mr. Jonson looked up and smiled. "Just a final inspection, then we'll run 'er up. Dave, I don't think you've met Kent—he's a friend of Bruce's."

Kent nodded carelessly at David and followed Mr. Jonson to the door of the airplane.

Mr. Jonson climbed into the cockpit and turned on the engine. Slowly the propeller began to revolve; soon it was just a blur, and the engine's roar filled the air. After several deafening minutes, he shut it off and jumped out. "Checks good," he said to Grandfather. "Okay guys, let's put this cowling back on."

He picked up the blue engine cover and dug a handful of screws out of his pocket. When the last screw was in place, he flipped his screwdriver into the red toolbox with a flourish. "Well, I guess we'll fly 'er and see how she does."

Mr. Jonson climbed back into the cockpit and took the little blue plane prancing across the pasture. When it paused on the other side, David knew that he was lowering and raising the flaps on the wings, checking them.

He tensed as the ghost of a memory wavered in front of him. Many times he'd watched his father checking his instruments in the same way. But he didn't want to remember.

He forced his mind back to the plane taxiing down the grass strip for takeoff. As it cleared the line of trees at the end of the field, Bruce let out a cheer. Then Grandfather smiled, Kent and Bruce clapped each other on the back, and suddenly everybody was talking at once. When the plane landed, David could tell from Mr. Jonson's broad grin that the test flight had been a success.

"Good," said Grandfather. "I think I might as well take her up. Anybody want to come for a ride? I can take two of you, for a start. Susan?"

"Oh, yes," cried Susan. "Could I? And David, too?"

His grandfather's indifferent gaze rested on him, and David drew back, feeling the cold sweat break out on his forehead. Riding in that plane was the last thing in the world that he wanted to do.

Hastily he turned to his aunt. "Why don't you go, Aunt Jeanne? I've been up lots of times before."

She gave him a surprised glance. "Well then, maybe I will. Do you think it's quite safe, Philippe?"

"Sure it is," Grandfather answered. "Bob Jonson is the best mechanic around. If he fixed it, then it's airworthy."

As the plane taxied away, David sensed the two boys beside him exchanging glances. But when he looked at them, Bruce avoided his gaze, and Kent's face was unreadable behind the mirrored sunglasses.

Suddenly David had to get away from the hangar. He strolled with elaborate casualness along the line of trees bordering the field. Maybe he shouldn't have backed off from that plane ride. Had Bruce noticed it? The look he'd given Kent could've meant something else. David's mind fastened on Kent. Bruce's friend was plenty sure of himself—David could tell that already. And there was something familiar about him too. Could he have seen Kent somewhere before?

He heard the airplane accelerate for takeoff and paused to watch it climb into the warm morning air. And then he was overwhelmed by memories of that other plane ride—in another country. It had been about seven years ago, just after his family had finished language study in France. Traveling in the small airplane with David were his mother and the baby, Susan. They were flying to meet his father, who had gone ahead to their new assignment, a mission station in North Africa.

When the plane crashed, he must have lost consciousness, because the first thing he remembered afterward was the screaming. It was the cry of a terrified baby—his little sister—and he wondered dimly why his mother didn't make her stop. He had pushed himself up painfully on one elbow to look around. Then he'd reached over to pat the baby, trying to shut out the horror of the airplane's wreckage. The baby had turned to him, holding up her soft, dimpled hands, and the crying had stopped. It seemed that he had been taking care of Susan ever since.

He shoved the memory of that day back into the dark corner of his mind where he wanted it to stay. Forget it. Forget it and get out of here.

Walking faster, he kept his eye on Grandfather's plane, now just the size of a bird, glinting silver in the sunlight. Since the day of the crash, he'd been afraid to fly in any kind of small plane. He hated to admit it, but that fear was still there; he'd felt it twisting his insides again this morning. And he couldn't seem to do anything about it.

He turned his back on the pasture and plunged into the woods, heading in the direction of the river. Wild vines snatched at his knees, sending him stumbling into the tangled snares of briars and fallen trees, but he didn't mind. It all helped in the forgetting.

Before long, he came upon a narrow path that was overgrown with weeds. He slowed his pace and slipped along it silently, trying not to disturb any animal or bird he might pass. The soft air enveloped him with mossy fragrance, and he felt the tension draining out of him into the stillness of the woods.

Noticing the bent stems of the tall grass ahead, he wondered if someone had used this path recently. Could it be the same path he'd seen branching off the main trail?

He followed it to the river, then walked downstream until he came to the fallen tree where he had found his stick. He perched on a limb, letting his gaze wander from the cool, silken water to the deep green trees in the river's wild border.

The peacefulness of this river . . . it was just what his father needed. Hadn't the mission doctor said that the best cure for his illness was simply to rest? David broke off a handful of twigs from the dead branch beside him and set them afloat. Dad wanted to do some writing for the mission during the long months that it might take him to get well. This would be the perfect place. Except that no one had suggested it. Why not?

Somewhere in David's chest, a chill began to spread. It was odd that neither Aunt Jeanne nor Grandfather had asked him about his father. And the one time that Aunt Jeanne had referred to him—when she was showing them the family tree—she had spoken as if Dad were . . . dead.

He stood up abruptly and brushed the fragments of bark from his lap. He'd had enough of wondering what was the matter. There was only one thing to do about it. Aunt Jeanne seemed to be more approachable than Grandfather. He'd talk to her and find out what was going on.

Chapter Six
A Puzzle in French

After lunch, when Susan had gone upstairs and Grand-father was painting as usual, David lingered in the kitchen, trying to find an opportunity to talk to Aunt Jeanne.

She was quite willing to tell him about her home in France, where she had grown up and married. After her husband had died, David's grandfather—a distant cousin—had suggested she come to the United States for a visit. She had accepted his invitation, deciding a few months later to stay and help raise his motherless son.

That was my father, David thought. Maybe now she'll talk about him.

But Aunt Jeanne fell silent, a faraway look on her gentle face as she dried her hands on a dishtowel.

"Come into the library," she said at last. "You have not seen the things from France."

In the library, sunlight shining through the tall windows made bright patches on the faded colors of the rug. His aunt stopped beside narrow shelves at the far end of the room and picked up a slender vase of pale blue glass. "This is lovely when you hold it up to the light," she said.

David nodded in agreement as the vase captured a sunbeam and glowed a delicate turquoise. "I like this statue," he said, sliding his hand over the bronze figure of a mounted knight. "He looks as if he's ready to charge into battle. Is it French too?"

"Yes," said his aunt. "That is very old, from the sixteenth century, my father told me. And so is this." Lightly she touched a round golden box, tracing the blue and white peacock feathers enameled on its lid.

As he looked around the room, David's eye was caught by a portrait that hung in a corner next to the shelves. Although the man in the painting wore side whiskers and an old-fashioned black waistcoat, he had the same dark, piercing gaze as David's grandfather.

"Is this one of our ancestors?" he asked.

"Yes," Aunt Jeanne answered slowly. "That was the Philippe who came to America."

"Where'd he get those pistols?" exclaimed David, stepping closer. He had seen flintlock pistols before, but not like the pair in the painting. They were small, perfectly matched, and looked as if they were made of solid silver. An intricate engraved design swirled along each curved handle, toward the silver trigger.

He heard a choked exclamation from his aunt. She turned away, murmuring, "If you will excuse me, I must . . . ah . . . we will talk again later, yes?" And she was gone, moving swiftly past the old leather chairs, leaving behind a faint scent of violets. David stared after her in bewilderment.

For a while he lingered in the library, examining the shelves of worn books, hoping that she would return. Finally he left too. Why had she run off like that? Was it something he'd done? He hadn't even asked her any of the important questions yet.

When he reached his room, he decided to begin the job of mounting the millipede he'd brought back from the river. Susan was napping—he'd seen her sprawled across the bed, her face flushed with the afternoon heat.

Sitting by the window to catch whatever breeze might be coming through the trees, he continued the job of smoothing down the butterfly net stick with his knife. To his surprise, he heard voices from the small porch below his window. Aunt Jeanne and another woman were conversing in swift French.

Only half-listening, because he'd forgotten a lot of his French, he skinned bark off the stick with long, steady strokes. Suddenly his knife faltered. They were talking about him. "*Le jeune* David. . . ." There it was again—his name—followed by a remark from Aunt Jeanne, who said how much he looked like his father. The other woman's voice agreed, and then she added something rapidly, repeating a certain French word several times.

Chairs scraped and the voices faded, as if the women had moved off the porch and into the house to continue their conversation. David puzzled over the French word they had repeated: *brouille.* He knew it . . . yes! It meant something like an argument. But how could an argument be connected with him?

He didn't hear Susan until she was halfway into his room. "Ready to go?" she asked with a yawn.

"Go where?" he answered, his mind still on that argument.

"Remember, you said you'd go down to the river with me this afternoon? Oh, it's so hot! Maybe it'll be cooler down there."

"Yeah," he said reluctantly. "Okay, let's go."

Once they were in the woods, David remembered the path he'd wanted to explore, and he showed Susan where it branched off the main trail. She pushed ahead of him happily, often disappearing into the bushes that hung across their way. David started thinking about the dark figure he'd glimpsed last night, and he remembered Kent's blond hair and black jacket. No wonder Kent looked familiar. Maybe that's who he'd seen on the trail—he could have been taking a short cut home through the woods.

The path led to the river, and they turned upstream, watching the water as they went. Today it rippled in gray wavelets that gleamed like polished silver. David stopped to examine a dead tree that had been drilled with hundreds of holes. "Look what the woodpeckers did, Susan," he said. "Instant pegboard!"

But she had wandered ahead of him, down the trail toward a clearing. Now she rushed back. "David, hurry up! I found the cutest little house, built right above the river."

He smiled lazily at her. "Won't it still be there if I don't hurry?"

"Oh, come on!" Her face glowed with excitement, and soon he understood why.

The clearing, ringed with tall spruce trees, seemed like a hushed, enchanted place out of a fairy tale. The gray stone building in the center had a small, pointed roof and was as round as a castle tower. It was encircled by its own tiny, paved courtyard.

"This must have been someone's summerhouse," David mused. Now it had an air of neglect. Shingles were missing from the pointed roof, and weeds had pushed up through the stones in the courtyard.

Susan cocked her head. "Something's making a noise in there."

David listened to a rustling from inside the house, and he grinned. Sounded like a great big scary squirrel. With Susan behind him, he followed the stepping stones that led to the courtyard and the open doorway. Together they peered inside.

It was empty, except for wind-blown leaves and a stone bench built into one curved wall. Above the bench, three simple windows provided a broad view of river and woods.

As David moved to take another step, the leaves under the bench stirred and a squirrel hurriedly backed out. It threw them a frantic glance, leaped to the low window, and disappeared.

Susan laughed. "What was he doing?"

"He probably hid a nut there last fall." David swished the rusty brown leaves aside with his foot, uncovering a small hole and freshly dug earth. "That's who was making your mysterious noise, anyway."

He kicked at the leaves again, and his foot caught the edge of one of the flat stones that paved the floor. The stone flipped up, revealing a wide, shallow hole. That squirrel really had been busy. Without giving it any more thought, he pushed the stone back into place. As he brushed through the crackling leaves, he noticed a cigarette butt caught between the stones. Looked like someone besides the squirrels knew about this place.

While Susan prowled around inside, David swung himself through one of the low windows, dropping lightly into the courtyard. It was bounded by a wide parapet of stone that formed a low wall. Three short pillars were set into the wall, all built of flat gray stone and patched with green velvet moss. A wild grapevine had grown over one end. It twined like thick, woody rope around the last pillar, as if to anchor it more firmly to the edge of the steep river bluff.

He stepped onto the stone wall to take a look at the strip of sandy beach eight feet below him. The river had cut deeply into the bank, exposing the tough, gnarled roots of an old willow tree that hung over the water.

"David?" Susan was curled up on the wide windowsill, her face dreamy. "What do you think this house was used for? Why is it here?"

"More questions, huh? I don't know." He'd been wondering about it, though. "Why don't you ask Aunt Jeanne? I've got questions of my own to work on."

"I will, then," his sister declared. "I'll find out, you'll see."

That night at the supper table, Susan hardly waited until everyone had been seated before starting into a colorful description of how they had discovered the stone house. She ended with the same questions she had asked David.

Surprisingly, it was Grandfather who answered. "Sounds as if you found the old summerhouse, Susan. It certainly has been there for a long time. Let's see. . . ." He glanced inquiringly at Aunt Jeanne, but she remained silent, with an uneasy expression on her face.

"It was built by my father as a birthday present for his bride." The stern lines of Grandfather's face relaxed. "She had her heart set on a shelter of some kind where she could sit and embroider and watch the river in the summertime. We used to call it her castle."

"It does look like part of a castle," agreed Susan.

"I haven't been down that way for some time," Grandfather said. "Is it still in pretty good shape?"

"Well, there are vines and weeds all over, but it looks okay," said Susan.

David had been watching Aunt Jeanne. Why did she look so upset? She must have noticed his scrutiny, for she flicked a sidelong glance at him and her face suddenly went blank. Then she turned away, making him wonder if she too disliked him.

After supper he retreated upstairs. He had work to do on his insect project and plenty of books to read. But it would be hard to settle down and study—to pretend that nothing was the matter in this strange old house.

As he stepped into his room, the gray cat slipped out from under his bed, arching her back in a graceful stretch. Then she leaped onto his quilt and sat watching him from slitted yellow eyes. He flung himself down on the bed to stroke her glossy back. At least he had her to keep him company.

"I haven't found out yet who you are, have I?" he said in response to her companionable purr. Then he remembered the questions he'd planned to ask Aunt Jeanne. He had hoped that maybe he could discover something about the argument that the two women had discussed. But the look on her face had warned him not to try. Not tonight.

The steady rhythm of the cat's deep purr lulled him into comfortable drowsiness, dulling his disappointment. There must be some way to find the answers he was looking for. He'd figure it out tomorrow.

The next morning at breakfast, Susan asked Grandfather if he was going to fly 55 Charlie again, and David listened uneasily. Next she'd be asking for another plane ride, with one for him, too. But Grandfather explained that the plane would be grounded for a while so they could give it a fresh coat of paint.

"Oh, good," said Susan. "What color are you going to paint it?"

"How about white and red?" asked Grandfather.

"That sounds pretty. With little stripes like Mr. Jonson's plane has? I like to paint too."

Grandfather laughed. "Those little stripes aren't as easy to paint as they look. Anyway, it won't get painted today. We've got to do a lot of work first."

David had a sudden idea. Perhaps if he did some work on the plane, he'd gradually lose his fear of flying in it. He spoke up quickly, before he could change his mind. "I'd be glad to help, if you can use me."

Grandfather's dark gaze flickered over him, as if he were surprised to find David there. "Well, yes. Kent helps out, but this will be a big job and there'll be things you can do. Why don't you ask Bruce and see what he thinks."

After breakfast, David went down to the hangar and found Bruce already at work. When he offered to help, Bruce's narrow, secretive face did not change, but he nodded. Then he explained, "The first thing we've got to do is protect the parts of the plane that might be damaged by the paint stripper. Then we'll strip off the old paint and give it a coat of primer. After all that, we can paint it."

Walking to the back of the hangar, Bruce said, "Let's start on the windows." He picked up a roll of shiny metal tape and showed David how to run it around the edge of the windows. Next, they cut up heavy brown paper and taped it in place over the windows.

While they worked, David felt Bruce's gray eyes studying him. It almost seemed as if he were trying to make up his mind about something, but he remained silent. When the windows were done, he handed David the roll of tape. "I'll start on the propeller. You can take this and do the door latches. Overlap it and make sure all of the chrome is covered."

David had almost finished twisting tape around one of the latches when a slim, black-haired girl ran into the hangar.

"Bruce, I got it! Nannette's going to let me use her bird book for as long as I want." She waved a thick blue book at Bruce, narrowly missing him as he stepped back to lift off the airplane's propeller. "You know what? This book has all kinds of diagrams. It shows barbs and barbules and—"

"Come on, Kelly, we're trying to get some work done," Bruce said impatiently. "I don't think David wants to listen to you and your big words any more than I do."

The girl must have caught sight of David standing by the airplane, for her face turned pink. And before he could say anything, she disappeared around the corner of the hangar.

He went back to his work on the door latch, but not without a stirring of curiosity. That was the same girl he and Susan had seen down by the river. He'd never met a girl before who talked about barbs and barbules. Those were scientific names he recognized—he'd learned them when he was studying birds. It might be interesting to get to know her.

Chapter Seven
The Letter Mystery

It wasn't long before David had finished taping the door latches and the fiber-glass antennas on the airplane. He was helping Bruce cover the wheels when Kent roared up to the hangar on a black motorcycle.

Bruce ran to meet the older boy outside, and after a whispered conversation they tramped back into the hangar. Kent raised his eyebrows at the sight of David, and he grunted something to Bruce while they started covering the airplane brakes.

For the rest of the morning David worked silently, conscious of being excluded, and he wondered about Kent's unfriendliness. By the time Susan came down to the hangar to call him for lunch, his fingers were stinging with small cuts from the sharp edges of the metal tape, and he was glad for a chance to stop.

As he left the hangar with Susan, they saw someone in a brown raincoat walking along the trail into the woods. "Who's that?" Susan asked in a low voice.

David was still thinking about Kent. "I don't know." He made his voice curt so she wouldn't ask any more questions. "Looks like an old lady. Maybe she lives around here."

During lunch, Aunt Jeanne must have noticed the dirty spots on David's pants, for she remarked to him, "I see you've been working on that airplane too. You'll ruin your good clothes with grease and dirt. Don't you have any old things to wear?"

Before he could explain that most of his clothes were stored back in New Jersey, she continued, "There are some old clothes in the attic that might fit you. They belonged to your father." She sounded bitter, and he wondered why.

After the meal was over, David followed her eagerly up a steep, uncarpeted flight of steps to the attic. Maybe now he'd get a chance to find out what was bothering her. When they reached the long, dim room, he held back his impatience while Aunt Jeanne gazed about as if she were in a dream. Dusty sunbeams from two narrow windows slanted toward the floor, gilding the ring of keys in her hand.

Finally she cleared a pile of dusty books off a wide black trunk. She unlocked it, lifted the lid, and stood there, staring at the clothes inside. Slowly she unfolded a shirt and held it up. As she measured it against David, her face softened.

"You look so much like him," she murmured. "That dark hair falling over your forehead, and the same serious brown eyes." Her voice faltered. "The night you came, I thought I was seeing a ghost from the past. "

Her mood seemed to change abruptly, and she turned from him, back to the trunk. "Here, check if these are long enough," she said in a flat voice. She handed him a stack of pants.

Obediently he held up a pair of brown pants against his own, but he was trying to make sense of her words.

"Yes, they'll fit," he said. "But I don't need all of these; just a couple of pairs will do." As he folded up the pants, the old clothes reminded him of something he needed for the insect trap he planned to make.

"You don't happen to have an old sheet anywhere, do you?" he asked. "I'd like to get one for a science project I'm working on."

His aunt glanced around the attic. "Oh, that's right, you are studying, aren't you? Susan said you are a scientist. Yes, I'm sure there's one somewhere."

She pushed past the trunk into a dark corner. "Look, you could use this old desk, couldn't you? It used to be your father's." She brushed at the dust on a small oak writing desk that had a hinged lid and a drawer below. "The last time I saw this, your grandfather had it in his studio, for painting supplies. He must have moved it in here."

She tugged at the drawer, which seemed to be stuck. David stepped over the trunk to help, and together they finally pulled it open.

"What are these?" she asked, lifting out two neatly tied bundles. "Letters?"

David leaned over to look at the envelopes and recognized his father's handwriting.

Aunt Jeanne, staring at the bundle in her hand, had recognized it too. "Letters from David?" she whispered. She snatched at the other bundle and clasped it to her. "All these years, I waited and waited. And I thought he never wrote." Her face twisted as if she were about to burst into tears. "Philippe must have put them up here—oh, how terrible!"

She stumbled toward the attic steps, and David watched her in surprise. "Take the clothes, and the desk too, if you want it," she said over her shoulder. "Later I will get the sheet for you."

Slowly David sorted through the scattered clothes and repacked the trunk, pondering what had happened. He'd always known that he looked like Dad. But why would that be such a shock to Aunt Jeanne when she first saw him? Was that what she had warned Grandfather about? More important, why had his grandfather hidden Dad's letters for all these years, obviously unopened? *What was wrong?*

There were no answers to his questions, so he set himself to the job of getting the desk out of the attic. He couldn't help feeling a glow of pleasure as he eased it down the stairs, one step at a time. A desk of his very own! And knowing that it had been Dad's made it all the better.

By the time Susan bounced in to see what he was doing, he had the desk dusted off and carefully positioned in the small back room. Then he listened to her questions while he arranged his specimens and books in it. But when he told her about finding the desk in the attic, he avoided mentioning the letters. Whatever had happened in this house, those letters from Dad seemed to be connected with it, and he didn't want his sister worrying.

Leaving Susan with a book, he wandered downstairs. Maybe Aunt Jeanne had read those letters by now and would tell him something about them.

At the open door of the library, he stopped. His aunt was sitting at the round table with the letters scattered in front of her. As he took a few hesitant steps closer, she jumped to her feet and swept the letters into a drawer.

"What's the matter?" he asked, shaken by the sight of tears on her face.

"The matter, it is terrible," she said, her English sounding very French. "Only if you could read these letters and talk to your grandfather—then maybe you would understand. . . . Oh, it is no use!" She gave David a despairing glance and hurried past him.

She started on down the hall, but a light tapping at the back door stopped her. Quickly she opened it.

"Ah, Nannette, I am so glad you have come!" she exclaimed. She hugged the small, white-haired woman who stood there, and poured forth a torrent of French that was punctuated by sobs.

When Nannette stepped into the hall, David recognized the old lady he had seen going into the woods. She answered Aunt Jeanne in French too swift for him to understand. Then, while he stood there feeling uncomfortable, she gently pried herself from Aunt Jeanne's embrace.

"*Alors,* Jeanne," she said in a low voice. "This is not kind to the boy." She gave David a penetrating glance from bright hazel eyes. "You must be the young David. Oh, and here is Susan."

David hadn't heard Susan come down the stairs. He wondered how long she had stood there and how much she had seen. She was smiling a small, polite smile, and her eyes were watchful.

"Let's sit down," Nannette said calmly, steering Aunt Jeanne into the kitchen. "We were just going to have a cup of tea, and you two must join us so we can become friends."

She moved assuredly about the kitchen while David's aunt sat back in a chair, her eyes closed. After Nannette had set a cup of steaming tea in front of Aunt Jeanne, she turned to David with a smile. "You would like milk, yes? And Susan, too?" Her friendliness took David by surprise, and all he could do was nod.

"And shall we have some cookies, Jeanne?" asked Nannette.

Aunt Jeanne waved toward a flowered jar on the counter, and Nannette filled a plate with plump chocolate cookies. "There now," she said, placing it in front of David and Susan. His sister picked up her milk and drank it silently, staring at Nannette as if she found her fascinating.

After a few sips of tea, Nannette put down her cup and spoke gently to Susan. "Your aunt and I are old friends." Her musical voice still had a trace of a French accent. "My name is Nannette, and I live in the white cottage in the woods. You'll have to come and visit me. Just follow the path that goes on up the hill."

She was interrupted by a scratching at the kitchen window. The gray Persian cat mewed plaintively at them through the screen.

"Ah, that rascal," exclaimed Nannette, getting up to open the window. "Of course she expects to come in too." The cat bounded into the kitchen, holding her tail like a feathery gray banner.

Susan glanced at David, wide-eyed. "Isn't that the cat who visits you at night?"

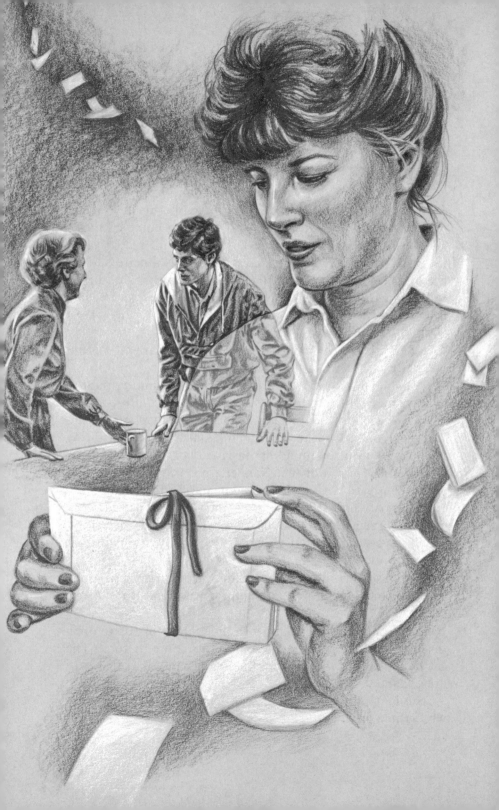

"Yes," he answered. "I've been wondering whose she is."

"Her name is Mimi—that means 'pussy' in French," said Nannette, stroking the cat. "She is most particular about her friends. You must be one of the favored ones."

David grinned. "Or maybe she just likes that room I'm in."

"That was your father's room, you know," said Nannette softly.

David looked at her with new interest. She must be the woman he had overheard talking to Aunt Jeanne. Perhaps he could ask her about the argument that somehow concerned his father.

But Aunt Jeanne quickly changed the subject. "Nannette was my dear friend and companion when I was growing up— my governess, you would say. When I moved here from France, I persuaded her to come with me."

David ate several more cookies while he listened to the two women talk. Apparently Aunt Jeanne had recovered her composure, and she steered the conversation toward subjects that had nothing to do with his father. Before long Susan was joining in, but David had lost interest.

Maybe I'll go down and see if Bruce needs some more help, he thought. He finished his milk and excused himself as politely as he could. On the way to the hangar he decided that he probably wouldn't learn anything more from Aunt Jeanne—every time he tried, she either got upset or avoided the subject. He'd have to talk to Grandfather. Tonight.

By supper time, David felt as if a rock had settled in the pit of his stomach. For some reason, the tender, browned pork chops didn't seem to taste very good. His mind kept jumping to the evening ahead. He had it all planned—he'd follow Grandfather when he went into the library to read the newspaper. And he would simply ask him if there had been some problem, perhaps some misunderstanding, concerning his father. That wouldn't be so hard, would it?

Aunt Jeanne handed him a piece of apple pie, but even for pie he had no appetite. Slowly cutting the sugar-studded crust into neat squares, he watched his grandfather eat, and he tried to banish the worry that kept surfacing at odd moments—about that policeman from the airport. Had he ever phoned?

At last Grandfather put down his fork and nodded to Aunt Jeanne. "A delicious meal, Jeanne, thank you." If he noticed that she had been quieter than usual during the meal, he did not comment on it. Nor did he look at David as he pushed back his chair and left the room.

"Excuse me, please," David mumbled. He hurried into the library.

His grandfather was gazing out a window at the far end of the long room, a newspaper folded under one arm.

"Grandfather?" His voice sounded squeaky and strange. He cleared his throat and began again. "Grandfather, can I ask you something?"

The man swung around to face him, and David gestured awkwardly at a nearby painting. "We had one of your pictures at Aunt Lucy's house. It was about the river, like this one, and had a big red paddle-wheel ferry in it."

"Yes, I know." His grandfather's voice was icily polite, his dark eyes unreadable.

David searched desperately for words. "My father told me about your being a painter, and I—"

"Dave!" Aunt Jeanne's face looked pale in the dimness of the library. She stood in the doorway at the far end, holding a white bundle in her arms. "Would you like to come and look at this?"

Reluctantly he left his grandfather and walked the length of the library to find out what she wanted.

"Here, I have the sheet you asked about, for the scientific project. How are you going to use it?" she asked.

"I was going to tear it into strips if you don't mind," David said hurriedly. "I'll paint it with a special sweet mixture to make a trap for the insects." He took the sheet from her, trying to think about what he would say next to his grandfather.

"Oh, yes?" She seemed to be keeping him here on purpose. "Would you need some molasses, perhaps?"

"Crushed bananas and molasses make a good mixture," he answered quickly. "They'd have to ferment for a few days first."

"I will get it ready for you, yes?" She gave him a nod and went off toward the kitchen.

David turned back to speak to his grandfather, but the library was empty, the door at its other end standing open. Swiftly his anxiety changed to anger. It seemed that Aunt Jeanne had deliberately interrupted their conversation. And then Grandfather had left, just like that.

He wadded the sheet into a hard ball and slammed his fist into it. This couldn't have anything to do with a policeman's report. Why didn't either of them want to talk about Dad?

Chapter Eight
Aunt Jeanne's Secret

Back in his room, David tossed the sheet onto his bed and paced the floor, trying to work off his frustration. Finally he paused by his open window, staring into the somber twilight.

A breeze whispered through the darkened trees, stirring their ragged tufts of needles. He inhaled the sharp scent of pine and remembered Nannette's words. This had once been his father's room. Suddenly he missed his father with an ache that was more than he could bear. He shoved his hands into his pockets to brace himself, and one hand nudged the smooth ivory of his knife.

He pulled it out. The engraved words leapt to meet his eyes: *Call unto me.* His Sunday school teacher had once said that he'd never be alone anywhere, that God would be with him. He could still remember verses about that, verses he'd learned for the contest.

He dropped the knife back into his pocket, feeling hollow inside. Even Bible verses didn't seem to be much help. That stuff was all right for Sunday school, but what good was it doing him now? He'd better get busy and figure a way out of his problems. Besides, it was Susan's bedtime.

Later that evening he began tearing up the sheet Aunt Jeanne had given him, and it gave him a grim sort of satisfaction to rip through the yellowed old cloth. He'd use four wide strips and one larger piece. There. Now all he needed was the sweet mixture. He'd ask Aunt Jeanne about it tomorrow. At least she didn't seem to mind his insect projects.

While he folded up the strips, his thoughts wandered to her sad words this afternoon: "Oh, it is no use." Was that why she hadn't wanted him to talk to Grandfather? What about the letters? Were they still down in that drawer in the library?

Maybe Dad's letters could give him the answers he'd been looking for. Why not go down and read them? Hadn't she said that he'd have to read them before he could understand? Then he would. He'd read those letters right now.

He picked up his flashlight and slipped through the room where Susan was sleeping, into the shadowy hall. The rest of the house was dark, except for a light in Grandfather's studio.

Silently he crept down the stairs, avoiding the creaky third step. What if Grandfather came down? David's stomach lurched, as if it had already happened. He didn't want to be the one who told Grandfather they had found the letters.

At the foot of the stairs he flicked on his light and followed its bright circle into the library. Had she locked the drawer of the round table?

No. It slid open smoothly, and he picked up a letter with eager hands. She hadn't put them back into the envelopes. No time now to arrange them in order.

Swiftly he began reading. His father began with news about his missionary work and then went on . . . wondering why he hadn't heard from them . . . loving concern and prayers. . . .

Another letter: a loving greeting . . . apologies for having left so hastily . . . a prayer for God to work in hearts so they could be together again. . . .

Yet another letter: something about a disagreement with Grandfather . . . about putting God first in his life . . . a mention of some pistols.

David looked up at the shadowy portrait of the long-ago Philippe Durant, remembering Aunt Jeanne's violent reaction when he'd asked about the silver pistols. What did they have to do with his father?

As he reached into the drawer again, he heard a faint creak from the stairs.

Instantly he switched off the flashlight and stood frozen, his heart hammering in the darkness. Someone was moving about. He could feel it, could sense it, although there wasn't another sound.

He jumped as a furry body brushed against him. The cat twined herself around his ankles with a throaty greeting, and he let out a long breath. Stooping to pet her, he whispered, "Mimi! I'm sure glad it's you. Did you find my open window? Wait a minute, I'm getting out of here."

Quickly he turned his light on and skimmed through the rest of the letters. They were mostly about his father's work, but he found one more reference to the silver pistols.

After returning the letters to the drawer, David slipped back to his room with the cat trailing him like a gray shadow.

As he lay in bed, the words written by his father paraded through his mind. There must have been a big disagreement between Dad and Grandfather. It sounded as if they were arguing about God, and there seemed to be some sort of connection with those pistols. After Dad had gone away, Grandfather hadn't answered any of his letters—hadn't even opened them. And he had never given them to Aunt Jeanne.

David eased the cat closer to him so that she was a fluffy, purring pillow under his hand. For a long time he stroked her, listening to the wind sighing in the pines and wondering what to do next.

Sunlight awakened him the next morning, and he bounded out of bed with renewed energy. Today he would get some serious work done on his insect study. No matter what his problems were, the deadline for that report remained the same. Besides, it was fun.

When Susan learned of his plans to map the trails around an ant colony, she begged to come along. "I'll just watch and not say a word, I promise," she declared.

"The day when you don't say a word. . . ." he muttered. It would be impossible to concentrate with her there.

"Listen, Susan," Aunt Jeanne suggested, "why don't you help me bake some cookies this morning? We can make the chocolate chip ones that you like, for our own tea party."

"Oh, good!" Susan exclaimed.

David allowed himself a small grin. "Don't eat them all."

"We'll save some for your brother, won't we?" Aunt Jeanne said, smiling at him. David was surprised at her concern. Now that he thought about it, she seemed different ever since—when? Since yesterday, when she'd found those letters from his father. Maybe it was important to her that Dad had written after all, and for some reason it had changed her feelings about him.

An hour later as he walked down the trail toward the river, his mind kept straying to the letters and the questions they'd raised. He brushed the questions aside and tried to think about finding an ant nest. What about under the tall maple trees over there?

He turned off the trail and climbed a bank laced with wild vines and small bushes. At the top of the hill he found a dry, sandy spot with the telltale holes he was looking for. He lay flat on his stomach to watch it. Ants were streaming in and out of a dozen holes, some trudging along with heavy loads and others marching away purposefully on unknown errands.

He was just reaching for his notebook when he heard a soft scratching in the bushes behind him. Quickly he turned toward the sound, and just as quickly, it stopped. As he waited, a blue jay swooped by, shrieking a harsh warning. Then he heard the scratching again, and with it, a feeble cry.

He jumped to his feet and parted the bushes, almost stumbling over a gray, furry body. Mimi lay with her eyes closed, panting. Bright red blood flecked the fur on her back.

Cautiously David knelt beside her, wondering if he dared touch her. "Mimi," he whispered, "have you been in a fight?" Her yellow eyes opened, and the pain he saw there spurred him to action.

"You're in bad shape," he said. "Come on, don't fight me. We're going to see Nannette."

He picked her up gingerly and started down to the trail. The big cat lay unresisting in his arms, and she seemed to grow heavier with each step. Finally he reached the white cottage. A neat stone path led him to the back, ending in a garden filled with masses of brilliant flowers.

Nannette was on her knees, weeding around a clump of yellow marigolds. Beside her worked Kelly, the black-haired girl who was Bruce's sister. She was the first to see him, and she jumped up with a cry. "What happened to Mimi?"

"I don't know," he told them. "I found her up on the hill. She looks like she lost a fight with something pretty big."

"Oh, poor pussy! Bring her in here," directed Nannette, leading the way to her small kitchen.

Gently David laid the cat on a towel Nannette had spread over the white table top. He watched in silence as she examined the cat's limp form.

At last she spoke, frowning. "This does not look like wounds from a fight. Her back is cut and bruised, as if she had been beaten. It is most unusual."

"Do you want me to call a vet?" David asked.

"A vet?" Nannette looked puzzled.

Kelly smiled at him in amusement. "Nannette is an expert at caring for injured animals." As if sensing his embarrassment, she went on quickly. "It's a good thing you happened to find Mimi. You probably saved her life."

"Yes," murmured Nannette, bending over the cat again. "It is a wonderful thing that you did."

Kelly's blue eyes sparkled at David. "What were you doing up in the woods there, anyway?" She waved at the burrs clinging to his jeans. "I can see that you weren't on the trail."

"I was mapping an ant colony," he said, watching for her reaction.

The blue eyes remained on his, bright and interested. "Really? That sounds like fun. Are you studying entomology?"

"Yes, that's supposed to be my summer assignment," he answered. "But it sounds to me like you're studying birds."

The girl flushed, and he couldn't tell whether she was pleased or embarrassed. "Well, sort of. How did you know?"

"Easy," he said with a grin. "When someone goes around talking about barbs and barbules—it's a dead giveaway." They both laughed at that.

He left an hour later, surprised that the time had passed so quickly, and he found that he couldn't forget his conversation with Kelly. It had been a long while since he'd laughed with someone his own age.

After lunch, he learned that a letter from his father had come for him in the morning mail. He scanned it hurriedly. Aunt Jeanne watched him with a worried expression on her face, and Susan tried to read it over his shoulder.

"What's he say? What's he say? Can I read it too?" she begged, hopping from one foot to the other.

"It says he's fine and he'll be leaving soon. You know you can't read his writing." David put on a smile for her benefit and changed the subject. "Did you hear what happened to Nannette's cat this morning?"

"No," his sister replied, her blue eyes alarmed.

"She got some cuts on her back—we don't know how. But don't worry, Nannette will take good care of her. Why don't you go over and see how Mimi is feeling this afternoon?" He looked appealingly at his aunt. "Do you think she could?"

"Certainly," Aunt Jeanne said. "Nannette loves to have visitors."

After Susan ran out of the house, happily banging the screen door behind her, David slumped back into the kitchen chair to reread his father's letter.

Aunt Jeanne asked, "Is it bad news, then?"

"No, not really," he told her. "My father must have written this as soon as he got the telegram about Aunt Lucy. He's feeling better. He's well enough to travel, actually, and he's coming to the States. He's been sick, you know."

Aunt Jeanne shook her head. "I did not know anything until I read those letters, and they are old."

David glanced up quickly. Maybe now he could find out something about the argument.

He chose his words with care. "The part I don't understand about this letter is that he tells us to meet him in Philadelphia when he arrives on Thursday. We're to bring all our stuff with us. It sounds as if he doesn't want to come here. Why is that, Aunt Jeanne?"

He watched the blood slowly drain from her face until her delicate features looked as if they were carved from ivory.

He leaned forward. "What's wrong? What has my father done, that you all hate him so?"

His aunt slid into a chair and covered her face with her hands. "I do not hate him," she said in a muffled voice. "I love him as my own son, as my very soul. Until I found those letters, I thought he had not cared enough to write to me. All these years I have prayed and waited for a word from me, and I . . . I grew bitter. And every time I looked at you, it was as if I were seeing him again."

She straightened up in her chair. "From those letters I learned that my David had written many times, and that he had not forgotten me." Her brown eyes filled with tears. "It is Philippe for whom I must pray now."

"But what happened? Why did my father leave?" persisted David.

Aunt Jeanne looked down at her tightly clasped hands for a long moment. Then she answered in a faltering voice. "They had a disagreement. It was terrible. Your father had set his heart on being a missionary, and he came here for one last visit before going to North Africa with his young wife. For a long time Philippe had opposed him, hoping he would change his mind."

She paused, and David waited, dreading what she might tell him about his father. "There is a pair of silver pistols, very old and beautiful, that was given to one of our ancestors by the king of France," she went on. "Another ancestor, Philippe Durant, brought them to St. Louis. Remember, I told you about him?"

David nodded.

"Those pistols have been handed down from father to son for generations, a symbol of the honor and courage of our family. On the last night that your father was here, he and your grandfather spoke together—I was with them in the library—and Philippe told David that he had dishonored the family by not respecting his father's wishes; and David said that he was sorry, but he had to obey God. Philippe swore that he would never give the pistols to him—*never!* He threatened to destroy them if David insisted on going to the mission field."

She took a shaky breath. "Philippe stormed out of the library. David turned to me and put his arms around me and said he must leave at once. He was white as death, and his poor wife was crying."

Aunt Jeanne shifted in her chair, and her voice faded. "Then there was a fire that night in the house, and the next day the pistols were missing." She fell silent, and David could feel the blood pounding in his ears.

Finally she added softly, "Philippe thinks your father set the fire and stole the pistols, but I know he didn't. Because I took them."

David stared at her in amazement, but she didn't seem to notice. "I probably set the fire too," she murmured, a dazed expression on her face. "Although that's not what Nannette thinks."

He sat still, hoping she would go on. When she didn't, he asked, "What did you do with the pistols?"

She gazed at him blankly. "I don't know."

Chapter Nine
The Silver Pistols

"You don't know?" David echoed, staring at her pale face in disbelief.

She sighed and ran a hand through her dark hair. "There was a great storm, with lightning and thunder. I think perhaps I went out to find a certain tree, for some reason. Then I . . . I fell on the path outside and hit my head. I can't remember anything more. When your father said he was leaving, I just—" She shook her head wordlessly.

The look she turned on David was haunted, full of pain. Impulsively he leaned toward her across the kitchen table. He had to do something to help. "Don't worry, Aunt Jeanne," he heard himself say. "This can't go on forever. I'm going to talk to Grandfather and get things straightened out, you'll see."

He could feel her watching as he left the kitchen and ran down the back steps, out into the searing sunlight. His feet carried him swiftly across the wide expanse of a pasture, and confused thoughts spun through his numbed brain, making no sense at all.

Finally, hot and breathless, he flopped down in the shade at the edge of the woods. For a long time he sorted painfully through the story of the missing pistols. Now he was getting answers to his questions, but they were answers that only brought more questions.

As his mind cleared, he recalled the promise he had made to Aunt Jeanne. He frowned, amazed at his own recklessness. He sure didn't want another confrontation with his grandfather. But it seemed like the only thing he could do. Maybe that was what Aunt Lucy had meant about being a peacemaker.

Okay, he'd get it over with—tonight he would talk to Grandfather. Slowly he got to his feet, wanting to do something that would take his mind off tonight. His notebook. It was still up by the ant colony; he'd go back and get it.

When he reached the anthill, he remembered the cat's injury. It would be interesting to see if he could find some clue to what had happened. He searched the small hilltop but saw only a few blood-smeared leaves.

At last he returned to the ant colony and turned to a fresh page in his notebook. *Friday, June 12,* he wrote in precise letters. *Ant colony, woods near St. Louis.* But the moment he started sketching ant trails, all the thoughts he had pushed to one side came tumbling back, destroying his concentration. Finally he gave up. Tomorrow he'd start over again. Everything would be better tomorrow, once he got this problem settled with Grandfather.

That evening after supper, when his grandfather walked into the library as usual, David was right behind him. As soon as Grandfather turned to pick up the newspaper from the round table, David began. "I had a letter from my father today."

Chilly silence fell like a wall between them.

He dragged out some more words. "Dad's been sick, so he's coming back to the States. He's arriving in Philadelphia Thursday night, and he wants us to join him there."

"Yes?" Grandfather's voice was like a door slamming.

David forgot his carefully planned speech and burst out, "Well, why doesn't he want to come here? He's been sick—he needs rest. This is his home."

Something came alive and burned in his grandfather's cold eyes. "Perhaps your father has not told you what happened here—what he did the last time he was *home*." The deep voice was heavy with sarcasm. "Don't you know that he took what was mine and ran like a coward?"

"Aunt Jeanne told me about it," David broke in, "but you have no proof. How can you condemn your own son without—"

"Proof?" The old man's thin lips tightened over the word. "Why do you talk to me about proof? The pistols are gone. Who else would take them?" He glared at David. "I know the story Jeanne made up to protect her precious boy. But where are the pistols? You bring them to me, and then we'll talk about proof."

Before David could answer, his grandfather added angrily, "And then there was the fire. He tried to cover up by setting fire to his own home, but he did not succeed."

Facts clicked coldly through David's mind. "There was an electrical storm that night," he countered. "It's not uncommon for lightning to set fire to a house like this one, built on a hill and surrounded by trees—especially pine trees. Take a good look at that stump by your back door."

His grandfather stared at him in surprise; then he shrugged. "Oh yes, you're the scientist, aren't you? At least you're different from your father. He couldn't do anything but stand there and chatter to me about obeying God." His face darkened as he remembered. "Maybe you aren't a fanatic like he is. Tell me, do you call yourself a Christian too?"

There was something frightening in his grandfather's look, but David lifted his chin stubbornly. "Yes, I am a Christian too. And you're wrong about my father." All at once David's icy calm deserted him. He tried to swallow the lump wedged in his throat, but it came right back, and there was nothing he could do but stalk out of the library and up the stairs to his room.

There he closed the door with precision, locked it, and dropped onto the bed with a groan. He felt as if something inside him had been shattered, leaving a hundred sharp, stabbing splinters. He buried his face in the pillow.

Philip Durant. All his life, that had been a magical name to him. He'd thought of his unknown grandfather as a wonderful person, shrouded in mystery. And here he'd turned out to be just a bitter old man.

Slowly David's dream of a happy home flickered and went out. Aunt Jeanne had been right. It was no use. The best thing he could do was leave, and the sooner the better.

From Susan's room, he heard Aunt Jeanne's soft voice as she read a story to his sister. Good, she was putting Susan to bed. He didn't want to see anyone tonight. It would be bad enough tomorrow.

Once he got into bed, however, he could not sleep, no matter how hard he tried. He stared into the warm, sticky darkness and listened to the melodious voice of the old clock in the hall.

Twelve chimes. Midnight here. In England it would be six o'clock in the morning. What would his father be doing now? How did he feel about the price he'd paid for obeying God? He'd never said. Did he miss the years that had been lost—no, stolen away—because of Grandfather's bitterness?

David rolled over, jerking the sheet loose. All those years! he thought indignantly. Years that Dad could have had a father's love and support . . . years that he and Susan could have had a real grandfather, instead of this stranger who seemed to have some kind of a grudge against God.

His grandfather's challenge rang in his ears. *Do you call yourself a Christian too?* David stirred restlessly. The answer had come automatically: of course he was a Christian. But he knew he wasn't the kind of Christian that his father was. Dad seemed to think about God all the time. He even talked about Jesus as if He were a close friend. David sighed. He heard the clock chime once again on the half hour before he fell into an uneasy sleep.

The next morning before David went down for breakfast, he made sure his grandfather had gone to his studio. Finding Aunt Jeanne alone in the kitchen, he apologized for being late. She gave him a sympathetic smile and scrambled some eggs for him while he poured a glass of milk.

"Where's Susan?" he asked, dropping bread into the toaster.

"She went down to the river with Kelly," his aunt said. "I think they're becoming good friends."

"I guess I'll spend the day working on my map of the ant colony," he said. "Do you mind if I don't come in for lunch? I'll just make a few sandwiches and take them along."

"That's fine," she answered. "I'll make you a picnic, so you won't have to leave your ants."

He smiled at her kindness, not wanting to admit the real reason that he wasn't coming back for lunch. Right now he couldn't stand the thought of seeing his grandfather again, of meeting those cold eyes. Until they could get away from here, he would avoid the old man as much as possible. He'd have to find out about getting to Philadelphia with Susan, too. But not now.

As he walked past the hangar, he kicked unhappily at a stick lying on the trail. The next thing he had to do was tell Susan. He was dreading that. She got along fine with Grandfather, and she loved her father dearly. How could he expect her to understand this conflict between them?

Turning off the trail, he climbed up to check on the ant colony. Perhaps he could do some work here while he was figuring out how to explain everything to Susan.

A blue jay glided past into the maple trees, dazzling him with a glitter of white and blue as he gazed after it. From the safety of a high branch, the bird stared back at him with bright, inquisitive eyes. It began singing a rusty-sounding song, and he felt his aching loneliness ease.

Today the ants were quieter, with only one or two workers strolling lazily in the morning sun. He took out the sugar Aunt Jeanne had given him and sprinkled it along the trails he'd noticed yesterday. In a few minutes dozens of ants came bustling out to investigate, and David reached for his notebook.

When the last grain of sugar had been carried off, he picked up his bag of lunch. Reluctantly he tramped down to the river. Green water shimmered in the sunlight, ripples blinking at him as the river hurried past. Now he had to find Susan and Kelly.

After walking for a short time along the edge of the high bluff, he saw them perched on a pile of tumbled rocks beside the water. He slid down a steep path to join them. Kelly had been drawing something, but she flipped her sketchbook shut as he approached.

Right away Susan began chattering, and David lounged on the sun-warmed rock, content to listen to her for the moment.

The sun caught the sheen of Kelly's glossy black hair as she turned to speak to him. "Well, how is the ant colony doing today?"

"Oh, they're busy little creatures," he answered, wishing he could think of something clever to tell her.

There was a short silence, embroidered by the trills of a cardinal from the woods above them. Then David spoke abruptly. "Susan, I came to tell you—we've got to leave—next Thursday."

His sister gazed at him in surprise. "Leave? Why?"

She intercepted his sidelong glance at Kelly, and protested, "Oh, Kelly's my friend. She won't tell any secrets."

But Kelly stood up and dusted herself off. "I'll see you later, Susan."

"Sit down, Kelly." David said it gruffly to hide his embarrassment. "There's no big secret. Your dad probably knows all about it anyway."

Swiftly he told them about the letter and the instructions from his father, and why they could never live here. By the time he finished, Susan was slumped against the rocks, and David could see the distress in her eyes.

"That's awful," she moaned. "I love it here—the river and 55 Charlie and Grandfather and Aunt Jeanne. We were going to make some Mississippi Mud Cake! Oh, David, I was hoping that Daddy could come here and we'd live here forever."

"I know, Susan," he said, heavy-hearted to learn that they'd both been dreaming the same dream. He flipped a pebble into the water, trying to think of a way to comfort her.

"Well, why don't you just find those old guns?" she demanded, sitting up suddenly. "If that's all the proof Grandfather needs, and we know Daddy didn't take them, they must be around here somewhere."

He sighed. Susan and her big ideas.

"You can do it," she persisted. "Remember, your science teacher told Aunt Lucy that you have such a good brain?"

He shook his head. "You've got to be kidding. Those pistols disappeared twenty years ago. I'm sure they've looked everywhere for them."

Kelly uncurled her long legs and picked up a small, flat stone. "People can be very haphazard when they're upset," she said shyly. "Maybe they never made a logical search." The stone spun from her hand to the river, making four perfect skips across the water. "Besides, it sounds as if your aunt has amnesia. That offers all kinds of interesting solutions."

He looked at her in surprise. He had forgotten that this girl was different from the giggling, mindless types he had known at school.

"You may be right," he admitted. Although Kelly's words made sense, he was still wary of Susan's enthusiastic plans. He couldn't tackle a project like this without doing some hard thinking.

In spite of his cautious reply, he suddenly felt better than he had for days. He eyed the brown paper bag beside Susan. "Is that the picnic lunch Aunt Jeanne packed for you?" he asked. "I've got one too. Why don't we eat while we discuss the possibilities?"

Chapter Ten
A Question for Nannette

They found a shady place at the edge of the river and sat with their backs against the sandy rise of the bluff.

"Aunt Jeanne really knows how to pack a lunch," Susan mumbled through a mouthful of chicken sandwich. She passed around pickles and hard-boiled eggs, and Kelly set carrot sticks and potato chips within easy reach.

David sat silently, letting his mind drift in aimless currents and eddies like the river in front of him. As he reached for another sandwich, he saw that Kelly was watching the river, a faraway look on her face.

Carefully he rehearsed what he would say to her, and then he tried it out loud. "What have you been doing these days, Kelly? You said you wanted to study birds. Were you sketching one just now?"

"Yes," she answered. "I took biology at school and got interested in birds, although I like any kind of science. Then I started visiting Nannette, and she knows lots of things about birds and wildlife. She paints them too. She said that drawing birds would help me learn about them more quickly, so she gives me lessons and I practice as much as I can."

She paused and they both watched a squirming brown-striped garter snake being rushed downstream by the current. "Whenever Bruce comes over to work on the airplane, I get a ride with him," she added.

"That reminds me," David said, "I'm supposed to help them in a while. I'd better not stay here too long." Inwardly he hoped that his grandfather would be painting this afternoon, not working on the airplane as he sometimes did.

"But we have to talk about finding those guns," Susan protested. "And this is Saturday. We've got to hurry and find them before Thursday."

"Okay, let's talk," David said. "Where do you think the pistols are?"

"How about asking Aunt Jeanne where she put them?"

"I told you, she can't remember. Do you know what amnesia is, Susan?" he asked.

She shook her head.

"It's a strange kind of forgetting. Usually it happens when a person has had a shock of some kind, and then they can't remember what happened, even when they try." He looked at Kelly for confirmation.

She nodded. "Their brain just sort of pulls a curtain over the things that are too painful to remember."

"Won't she ever remember?" asked Susan.

"Sometimes the memories come back, but after twenty years it doesn't look very promising," David said.

"You know what? Nannette must have been living here at that time," said Kelly reflectively.

"Come to think of it, when Aunt Jeanne was telling me she must have set the fire, she said that Nannette didn't think so," remarked David.

"Yes, and she might know something that Aunt Jeanne left out. She was very fond of your father."

"Does she talk to you about him?" asked David.

"Only a little," answered Kelly. "She told me how much you look like him and talk like him."

"Yes," Susan put in. "I heard Nannette say that even though you look so gruff and serious, you're really a friendly person underneath." She smiled innocently at Kelly. "He is, isn't he?"

"I think I'd agree with that." Kelly slanted a mischievous grin at David, and he felt his face grow hot.

But Kelly was already changing the subject. "How did you get started on a project in ants this summer, anyway?" she asked calmly. She got to her knees to pick up the sandwich papers and then handed out chocolate chip cookies.

Eagerly David told her about his interest in science, and he described the remarkable man he'd had for a science teacher. As he relaxed, the words came more easily and he found himself enjoying the conversation with her, stopping occasionally to answer a question from Susan.

Finally he glanced at his watch and got to his feet. "I'd better get going or Bruce will give up on me. Maybe I'll have a chance to talk to Nannette soon. See you later."

When he reached the hangar, he found that Kent was there too, helping Bruce smear a thick, amber-colored liquid onto the old blue airplane.

Bruce explained what they were doing. "This paint stripper works pretty well, but it takes forever. You can see we didn't get much done yesterday. If you want to help, you can go back to the workbench and get yourself some gloves and a couple of those orange pads to scrub the bad spots with."

When David stepped past the bench, his foot struck something that spun twinkling into a corner. He picked up a small steel ball that was about the size of a BB, and as he dropped it into his pocket, he noticed a scattering of brown spots on the cement floor. It looked like dried blood.

"Hey, is that blood on the floor over in the corner?" he asked Bruce curiously.

"Blood? Yeah, maybe," Bruce said. "Kent and me got us a squirrel back there the other day with our slingshots. Now, see how this paint is bubbling up? We wash it away with the hose, like this." He directed a powerful stream of water at the door of the plane and it turned to dull silver as the paint washed off. "Okay. Take a pad and get the stuff that's left, around the rivets."

It wasn't long before David understood what to do, although he felt awkward beside Kent's quick, silent efficiency. Finally the older boy pulled off his rubber gloves and threw them onto the workbench. "I'm going," he said to Bruce, pushing blond hair out of his eyes. "See you at Tom's place later on—he's got some good stuff." He sent David a mocking glance and strode out of the hangar.

After Kent had gone, it seemed as if something dark and menacing had left with him. David found that Bruce was more sociable and talkative now that they were alone.

"Are you and Kent pretty good friends?" he asked.

"We sure are," Bruce answered in a proud voice. "He's real nice to his friends. Sometimes he even lets me borrow his motorcycle." He gave David an encouraging grin. "Don't let him get under your skin. It usually takes him awhile to decide if he likes a guy. He was asking me if you'd said anything about seeing him somewhere before."

"Maybe," David answered. "I think I saw him in the woods the other day."

Bruce turned the hose off and dried his hands. "Well, that's all I'm going to do for now. We can pick it up tomorrow. Kent'll be here to help too."

Taking his jacket down from the nail where it hung, he pulled a metal slingshot from the pocket. "This little beauty is more fun than a barrel of monkeys. I can put away a squirrel or a rabbit with just one shot in the right place."

He centered a small steel ball in the leather strap of the slingshot and took elaborate aim at a distant tree. Then he grinned, lowering the slingshot. "Birds are fun too, but I lose too much ammunition with them." He flicked a sideways glance at David. "Do you want to try it? That blue jay in the tree over there has been askin' for it all afternoon."

David remembered the flashing blue grace of the bird he had admired this morning and pictured it lying on the ground, spattered with blood.

"No, that's okay," he said hastily. "I've got to get up to the house for supper. You don't happen to know if my grandfather is home, do you?"

"I doubt it. He went over to the airport this afternoon. The skydivers needed a pilot and Dad was busy." Bruce gave David a quick glance. "You look like you're glad he's gone. Did you two have a fight?"

"It's not us, exactly," David said slowly. "I just found out about some kind of trouble between him and my father that's been going on for years. A family heirloom disappeared, and he thinks my father took it."

"Boy, you've got a problem there," said Bruce. "I like your grandfather, but he sure is stubborn. Once he gets an idea. . . ." He shook his dark head sympathetically at David. "If you get any good clues where it is, tell me and I'll help you look."

"Thanks, Bruce," David said. "See you tomorrow."

On his way up the path to the house, he passed Nannette walking in the opposite direction. She gave him a friendly smile.

"How is Mimi today?" he asked.

"She is much better. Why don't you come for a little visit after supper tonight, and you can see for yourself?"

"Okay," he answered. "I'd like to do that."

With an affectionate nod, she turned and started into the woods toward her cottage.

David looked after her, making plans. If Aunt Jeanne would keep Susan at home, tonight might be his chance to ask Nannette about the missing pistols.

After supper Susan willingly helped Aunt Jeanne with the dishes, and David slipped out the back door. He found Nannette in her garden, digging around a clump of starry-eyed daisies.

"Hello, young David," she said, straightening up slowly. "Are you familiar with this herb?" She bent one of the bright daisy clusters toward him. When he shook his head, she explained, "It is called chamomile, a very good herb for tea. Come in and I will make some for you."

Nannette's small kitchen had bunches of plants that looked like dried flower stalks hanging from the ceiling. The air was filled with a subtle fragrance, and he wondered about it while he petted the cat. Somewhere, he had smelled that scent before.

Meanwhile, Nannette had washed her hands and set a shiny kettle of water on the stove. From a jar she scooped up a spoonful of tiny dried yellow flowers and dropped them into a red teapot.

"Mimi sure does look better," David commented as the cat hobbled over to her dish of food. "Do you suppose she'll be able to run and jump as well as she used to?"

"I think so," Nannette said, but there was a pucker of worry on her forehead. "The cuts are healing well. I am hoping the hindquarters are not crippled. No bones are broken there, but the nerves may be damaged. She was terribly bruised."

David thought about Bruce's slingshot and wondered if he should mention his suspicions. But why upset Nannette when he wasn't sure? Now she was smiling down at the cat, who crunched steadily at her food. "Mimi is eating better, too," she said. "We'll just have to wait and see."

Nannette poured boiling water into the teapot and set two blue-flowered mugs on the table. "Sit down now," she said in her brisk way. "Tell me what has been troubling you."

"What makes you say that?"

"Your father used to get the same dark look, like a thundercloud on his brow," she replied calmly. "You have been talking to your grandfather, haven't you?"

"Yes, I found out about the argument between him and my father," David answered, relieved that she was willing to discuss it. "Aunt Jeanne said she's the one who took the pistols and set the fire. But she can't remember anything about it. Do you think she has amnesia?"

"That could be," agreed Nannette. "It's easy to understand why. She had raised your father from a child. She loved him very much, and your grandfather as well. It was unbearable for her to hear Philippe's angry words and then have your father leave like he did."

"Why did she take the pistols, anyway?"

"Who knows?" Nannette lifted her shoulders in a delicate French shrug. "Your grandfather had threatened to destroy them, and after all, they are an heirloom that has been cherished by the family for generations. You may have noticed that she is interested in the family tree and such things."

"Yes," David agreed. "She showed me some French antiques in the library."

"It's a strange thing about your aunt," Nannette continued. "That night, when I found her lying on the path, she seemed to be in a trance. Perhaps it was shock. I had seen the flames of the burning house and was on my way over to help. I almost stumbled over her. She was a sight—all soaking wet from the rain—and I helped her to sit up. She just sat there, clutching at the moonstone brooch on her blouse."

David leaned forward, intent. "Was she carrying anything?"

"I found her knitting bag on the path beside her, but it was empty. Later we noticed that one stone was missing from the brooch, but that wasn't surprising, because the stone had been loose."

Nannette poured a steaming liquid from the teapot into David's cup, and he gazed doubtfully at the clear golden tea. It had a warm, grassy fragrance that reminded him of a summer meadow.

"Just sip it at first," advised Nannette, handing him a teaspoon.

David sampled a small spoonful of the tea. "It tastes like it smells," he said. "Different. But sort of pleasant," he added politely. He thought of another question. "What do you think caused the fire?"

"There was much lightning with the storm that night, and it came very close to the house," Nannette said. "Ever since then, Jeanne has been terrified of thunderstorms."

David nodded. That made sense. "You said Aunt Jeanne was wet. Did she run outside without a raincoat?"

"No, she is sure she must have put on her raincoat, but she can't remember. After the argument, it is just a blackness in her mind, she says. We never did find her coat."

David took another cautious sip of his tea. "My problem is that I think it's hopeless and we might just as well leave. But Susan has this big idea that I can find those pistols, and then we'll live happily ever after."

Nannette nodded. "It is a difficult decision. Have you asked God what He wants you to do?"

David flinched from her bright gaze. He knew he couldn't hide his doubts from this unusual old lady who seemed to know him so well. "What does God have to do with it?" he asked, feeling the need to defend himself. "And what does He care, whatever I do?"

Nannette's voice was firm, confident. "God does care about you. He even has a plan for your life."

"People keep telling me that. But how can I be sure? What kind of care did He take of my mother? And just look at my father!"

"What does your father have to say about it?" she asked gently.

"Well, it doesn't seem to bother him," David answered in annoyance. "He keeps saying things like, 'All things work together for good.' But I don't have his kind of faith. Grandfather calls it fanaticism."

Nannette sighed, and the smile lines on her face fell into wrinkles. "I know what your grandfather calls it. For many years I have prayed for him and for your dear father. Now I will pray for you."

She glanced at the dusk gathering outside the windows. "It is getting late. You should probably go now, although I have enjoyed our visit. When I wrote your Aunt Lucy that letter, I wondered if it was wise to encourage you to come here. But now I think that it was part of God's plan."

So the letter had been from Nannette. David took another look at the dried flowers above his head, finally recognizing the pungent scent of lavender. He smiled at her. "Whatever happens, I'm glad you sent that letter."

He was rewarded by the twinkle in her eyes as she walked with him to the end of her steppingstone path. "Why don't you ask Jeanne to show you her moonstone pin?" she suggested. "It may help you to understand what happened that night. Will you come again soon?"

"Sure," David promised.

He had just turned onto the main trail when he met Susan waving her flashlight at him.

"Oh, I was looking for you. Did you go see Nannette? Is Mimi better? Will you read me a story tonight?" She paused for breath and he had to laugh.

"Yes, yes, and yes. If you don't ask me any more questions."

"But I thought you liked to explain things, Mr. Scientist," she said pertly.

David grinned. "Take it or leave it," he told her.

After that they walked in silence through the densest part of the woods, where twilight was thickening fast. From the corner of his eye, David glimpsed a shadow trailing them through the trees. This ought to be interesting, he thought.

"Hand me that flashlight," he whispered to his sister.

Chapter Eleven
The Moonstone Pin

"What's the matter?" Susan asked.

"Shhh," David cautioned. "Hasn't anybody warned you about the grizzly bears in these Missouri woods?"

He flashed the light in the direction of the stealthy figure, and for a minute all they could see was a pair of eyes glowing red through the gloom.

Susan stopped short. As the eyes disappeared, she giggled. "I don't know what that is, but it's sure no grizzly bear."

David chuckled. "Mimi?" he called.

The eyes appeared again, and blinked. "Mimi!" He switched the flashlight off, and the shadow limped toward them.

"It *is* Mimi," Susan cried. She ran to pet the cat. "Did you hear him try to tell me you were a grizzly bear? You should scratch his nose for that! Off you go now—I'll see you tomorrow."

When she rejoined David on the path, she asked, "Why do her eyes do that anyway?"

"It's called night shine," he explained. "There is a special patch of cells in the retina of her eye. It acts like a mirror

and reflects light. Cats and a lot of other night prowlers
have it. Her eyes looked like neon lights, didn't they?"

"They looked weird," Susan remarked. "I'm glad there's
a scientific explanation for it."

That night while he took a shower, David considered what
Susan had said. Scientific explanations *were* satisfactory, like
science itself. There was usually a logical, reasonable answer
there; all you had to do was find it.

But what about the pistols? Was there a chance of his
ever finding them? His mind filled with haunting pictures:
his father's pale face, Aunt Jeanne's shadowed eyes, Susan's
eager, pleading smile.

He had to try, at least. He could talk to Aunt Jeanne,
perhaps get her to tell him some more about that night and
ask her about the moonstone pin. Perhaps her amnesia would
improve. There was a chance.

He went to bed and slept soundly, encouraged by his
own determination.

The next morning when David went downstairs, purposely
late again, he found Susan and Aunt Jeanne in the kitchen
just finishing breakfast.

"You sure are a sleepyhead," Susan teased him. "I've been
up for hours. I had breakfast with Grandfather first. Did
you know he eats breakfast at six o'clock so he can get to
his painting early? Then I ate another breakfast with Aunt
Jeanne." She sighed in contentment.

In the next breath she asked, "What are you going to
do today? Oh, I forgot, it's Sunday, isn't it?" She gazed at
her aunt curiously. "Aren't you going to church? We always—"

"Susan—" David muttered.

"I'm sorry. I didn't mean to be rude," his sister said hastily.
"Maybe you don't have a church around here."

"It's all right," Aunt Jeanne reassured her. "There is a
church that Nannette and I usually go to, and Kelly has
been coming with us. But the lady who picks us up is sick
today. Perhaps another time we'll all go together, yes?"

"Oh, I see," said Susan, satisfied.

Guilty relief pricked through David. Somehow, the thought of going to church today made him feel uncomfortable. But would there be another time? Where would he and Susan be next Sunday? Soberly he set about helping himself to breakfast.

After Susan had wandered out onto the porch, Aunt Jeanne poured herself another cup of coffee and sat down at the table across from him.

"I had a good visit with Nannette last night," he told her. "We talked about the pistols." He slanted a quick glance at his aunt, who was staring at her coffee cup. "She mentioned that you have a moonstone pin and that part of it was lost."

"Yes," Aunt Jeanne said softly. "My husband gave it to me when we were first married, as a symbol of our love." She drew her brows into a thoughtful frown. "There was a tree down by the river that. . . ." Her voice faded, and she shook her head. "Oh, I don't know."

She reached for her coffee, but the delicate blue cup clattered in its saucer, and he saw that her hands were trembling. Abruptly she rose from her chair. "I will show you the brooch."

He had finished the rest of his eggs and was slicing more bread for toast when she returned.

She laid a small brown leather box on the kitchen table. "Here it is. Keep it for as long as you like." She paused, groping for words. "It . . . it reminds me of that terrible night, and now that one of the stones is gone, I do not like to see it very much." Looking solemn, she left him alone.

He put down the bread knife, wiped his hands on his jeans, and opened the box.

The antique gold brooch held a silhouette of two trees outlined in gold against a gleaming river of blue enamel. It looked as if the pair of golden trees were growing into each other, for their roots and branches were closely intertwined. Within the twisted tree roots was set a single round moonstone, shimmering and lustrous. Beside it gaped the blank space where its twin must have been.

David spread jam on his toast and ate it while studying the strangely linked gold trees. Suddenly he stopped chewing. What had Aunt Jeanne said about a tree down by the river? Didn't amnesia victims sometimes have a flash of memory?

Quickly he cleared away his breakfast dishes and Aunt Jeanne's cup of cold coffee, thinking about his new idea. Perhaps, years ago, his aunt had found a tree beside the river that reminded her of the trees on the moonstone pin. Maybe she had run down there that night, and for her own private reason had hidden the pistols in the tree. It was worth investigating.

He slipped the brown box into his pocket and hurried through the woods to the river. When he paused at the high bank overlooking the water, he saw Bruce trotting down the trail toward him.

"Hi, Dave," he called cheerfully. "Any luck finding that missing family heirloom?"

When David shook his head, Bruce asked, "What is it, anyway? A diamond necklace or something like that?"

"Not exactly," David answered. "It's a pair of silver pistols. I guess they're antiques by now."

Bruce's gray eyes widened. "Now that's what I call an heirloom. They'd be worth thousands today, I bet." He scratched at the sparse black hairs of his moustache. "Were they still in the case?"

David looked at him curiously. "What do you mean?"

"Most of those old guns were kept in a wooden case— specially made to protect them from moisture and stuff."

"I don't know if there was a case," David said slowly, "but that's a good idea. I'll have to ask Aunt Jeanne."

"Yeah. Well, I'm going down to work on ol' 55 Charlie."

"Okay, I'm coming over to help you after a while. Think we can finish the stripping today?"

Bruce nodded. "Hope so. See you later."

After Bruce had disappeared into the trees, David took the moonstone pin from his pocket and examined it again.

Was he looking for two trees growing together, or one tree with a split trunk? He'd just have to keep his eyes open.

Slowly he walked up the river, studying the trees as he went. There were several oddly shaped trees, but none that suited his purpose. He had almost reached the summerhouse when he found Kelly sitting on a large rock beside the water, writing in her notebook.

"Hi!" She smiled up at him. "Hunting for insects? If you're down here looking for mayflies, you can see them better tonight."

"I wasn't looking for—" David interrupted himself. "Did you say mayflies? I've read about them. I'd sure like to get a couple for my collection."

"Come back down to the river at sunset, and you can get hundreds of them," she said. "They swarm all over this time of year. Willow bugs, we call them."

"Maybe I'll do that." The bulge in his pocket reminded him about the moonstone pin, and he sat down to show it to Kelly. He told her about what he had just learned and his idea that Aunt Jeanne might have hidden the pistols in a tree somewhere along the river.

"I know she never comes down here anymore," Kelly remarked. "It must be awful for her to have those memories locked up inside her head. No wonder she looks sort of haunted sometimes."

"That's what I thought when I first got here," he said. "Twenty years is a long time to wonder about—" He stopped and shook his head. "Oh, no."

"What's the matter?"

Gloomily, David snapped the jewel box shut. "Do you realize what a dumb thing I've been doing? Walking along, looking for a tree that was here twenty years ago! It could have been cut down, blown over. . . ."

"Or swept away by the river," Kelly murmured, looking at the swift green water beside them.

"It's probably long gone. And Bruce was just telling me that those guns were usually stored in a wooden box. So if she dropped it out here somewhere, it would be just a pile of rotted wood by now, anyway."

He stood up, feeling disheartened. "I'm sure not a very good detective. I guess I'd better get down to the hangar and help Bruce. Might as well forget my great idea."

But Kelly remained where she sat, staring across the river. As David watched, a look of deep sadness crossed her face. He sat back down beside her. "What are you thinking?"

"It just reminded me, what you said about Bruce. I'm so worried about him."

"About Bruce?" he asked in surprise.

"Yes, he's got some kind of a complex, and I'm afraid it's going to get him into trouble. See, he's not very tall, and when he compares himself to Dad, he probably feels like a runt. Dad's sort of the overpowering type."

She flickered a sideways glance at David. "It sounds silly, but I think Bruce keeps trying to prove something—that he's as good as the kids who are bigger and stronger than he is. Like Kent Harper."

He nodded. "I can understand that."

"Well, lately he's been a lot worse. Maybe it's from working on that airplane with Dad so much. Or maybe it's Kent and that new bunch of kids he runs around with." She shook her head. "Seems like all he can talk about is wanting money."

"Lots of kids think they'd be happy if they were rich," he said thoughtfully.

"Yes, that's what they think," she retorted. "But I never was really happy until I accepted Christ as my Saviour." David glanced at her in surprise and saw that her eyes were glowing.

"Nannette helped me to understand about Him a couple of months ago," Kelly went on, "and Jesus Christ is the best friend I've ever had. I wish Bruce could know Him."

With a sigh she added, "I tried to tell Bruce about Christ, but you know what brothers are like. He just doesn't take me seriously."

She turned to him with a hopeful smile. "But you could talk to him, couldn't you? Maybe he'd listen to you."

David lowered his gaze before the blazing intensity of those blue eyes. How could he tell her that right now he felt about a million miles away from God? He picked up a ragged leaf and tore it to shreds.

"Well, you're a Christian, aren't you?" Kelly faltered. "And your father's a missionary and everything. . . ." Her voice was low and pleading. "David?"

"I don't know." He almost choked on the words because his throat was aching. "I'm not sure of anything anymore."

He stole a glance at her and saw that the light in her eyes had faded.

Suddenly he was on his feet, murmuring an excuse. He turned and walked swiftly down the river path, not daring to look back.

Chapter Twelve
Dance of the Mayflies

When he reached the hangar, David found that Mr. Jonson was there with Bruce and Kent, helping them finish the stripping process on the airplane. He welcomed David in his boisterous way and soon had him working so hard that there was no time to think. David was glad for the work; he didn't want to remember Kelly's stricken face.

But he was reminded of her worries about Bruce when he noticed what a contrast Bruce was to his big, heavily muscled father, and how short he looked beside Kent's tall figure. Mr. Jonson's comments, delivered in his booming voice, did seem unnecessarily critical at times.

Just before noon, they washed off the last of the paint stripper, and Mr. Jonson surveyed the airplane with approval. "We'll let her dry this afternoon and spray the primer on tonight."

It felt good to have had a part in finishing such a big job, but David's satisfaction faded as he scrubbed his hands for lunch. Grandfather would be at the table, and now there was no way he could avoid him.

As he walked into the dining room with Susan, he listened absently to his sister's account of Nannette and the cat. From the kitchen came the voices of Aunt Jeanne and his grandfather, speaking in French.

He heard the low question, "How is the boy today?" and Aunt Jeanne's answer, "He is still upset." Then the two entered the dining room, and David, feeling their eyes upon him, held his face carefully expressionless.

Susan kept up a lively conversation with Aunt Jeanne throughout the meal, and for once he was glad for her chatter. Grandfather remained silent, his face stern and remote, as if he had retreated into another world. David watched him guardedly. Why had Grandfather even bothered to ask Aunt Jeanne about him, anyway?

After lunch, rather than spend an afternoon alone with his thoughts, he asked his aunt if she had any chores that needed to be done. Her warm brown eyes rested on his face sympathetically, but she did not ask the reason for his offer.

"Yes, there is certainly something you could do. Today I was feeling so sorry for my rose garden—it is just choked with weeds. Would that be a very bad job?"

"I can do it," he declared. "And Susan will help too." He had to grin at the indignant look his sister threw him. "C'mon, with all the baking and tasting you're doing, you'll be as fat as a butterball if you don't get some exercise."

As he stepped out onto the back porch, his gaze fell upon the charred tree stump. Now that he knew it had been burned on the night of the fire, the ugly blackened hulk was a reminder of his grandfather's bitterness. He avoided it and hurried toward the tool shed.

Although the heat hung thick and heavy over Aunt Jeanne's garden, David found a certain release in swinging savagely at the weeds with the hoe, as if he could root out his own problems that way. While he worked, he explained the function of plant roots to Susan. He was just getting to photosynthesis, the interesting part, when a shadow fell across the ground in front of him. He brushed the perspiration from his face with his sleeve and looked up.

His grandfather stood there, holding two glasses of lemonade. "Thought you might be ready for a break," he offered.

Susan jumped up with a glad cry, took her lemonade, and sprawled in the shade to drink it in noisy gulps.

"Thanks," David mumbled. The sweet, tangy liquid tasted wonderfully cool, in spite of his uneasiness at seeing Grandfather there.

"Bob Jonson said you've been a big help with the plane," his grandfather remarked as they joined Susan in the shade. "Are you and Bruce getting to be pretty good friends?"

David nodded, and Susan interrupted, "I sure hope you don't get too friendly with that Kent. He makes me feel spooky."

"I don't know Kent very well," Grandfather said, "but I've always thought that Bruce seemed to have a lot of ability. Now that he's finished high school, he wants to earn his mechanic's certificate and then get a job flying with the airlines."

He smiled at Susan as she handed him her empty glass. "How did that taste?"

"Great!" She turned and frowned at the weeds that remained. "Almost done." She sighed. "David, if I have to listen to one more science lecture, I'm going to die. Can't we leave photo-whatever-it-is for another day?"

It was Grandfather who answered. "Keep your ears open, Susan. You might learn something."

She groaned good-naturedly. David was not certain, but he thought he saw a twinkle in his grandfather's eyes as he left them.

He went back to work, trying to sort out his confused feelings as he slashed at the last few clumps of weeds. He had to admit that his grandfather wasn't really such a terrible person. He was kind to Bruce, for instance, and he'd comforted Aunt Jeanne during the storm. But how could he be so heartless about his own son? Was it because his son had chosen to obey God instead of him?

David kicked the last weed loose and tossed it into the bucket for Susan to empty. "That's it, kid; see you inside," he called over his shoulder. After putting the hoe away, he went into the house to cool off with a shower.

But the rushing water only reminded him of the river and of what Kelly had said. Sure, he'd been a Christian for years, although he couldn't talk about Christ like she did. What was the matter with him, anyway? And why did he feel so far away from God?

While he pulled on some clean clothes, he eyed the collecting jars on the bureau, remembering that he'd wanted to go down to the river and catch mayflies. Right after supper would be the best time.

From the bedside table, he picked up the small leather box and held it, hesitating. It might be a dumb idea, but he couldn't help feeling that having the pin along might help him figure out what Aunt Jeanne was thinking when she hid those pistols.

His mind made up, he tried to fit the box into a pocket, but it was too big for any of the pockets in this fresh pair of jeans, so he unpinned the brooch from its brown velvet bed. As he held it up to the light, the pale moonstone sprang to life, its depths pulsing with an eerie blue glow. If only it could tell him the secrets of that stormy night!

Carefully he wrapped it in a piece of tissue paper and slid it into his right-hand pocket, remembering that the other one had a hole in it.

Although he left immediately after supper, by the time he reached the river the sun was hanging low over the water, and its long, slanting rays were turning the ripples to gold. He scrambled down the steep bluff to the water's edge. Before starting to hunt for mayflies, he wanted to check this area for trees like the ones on the moonstone pin. Now he would look for tall giants, however, or even dead old snags.

He dug down past the pillboxes in his pocket for the pin. Unwrapping it, he cradled it in his palm to study once more. There must be some special feature to those trees;

something he was missing. He gazed at it, fascinated, as the brooch shone in the sunlight with the rich sheen of old gold, and the moonstone breathed its mysterious fire.

Over his shoulder he saw Bruce approaching, and he quickly closed his hand over the pin.

"Hi, Dave. What you got there?" Bruce threw a curious glance at his hand.

For some reason, he was reluctant to show Bruce the pin, but he slowly opened his fingers.

"Hey, that's pretty! Where'd you get it?"

"It's Aunt Jeanne's." He tried to explain. "I was hoping it would give me some ideas about finding the pistols."

"If she ever wants to make some money on it, let me know," Bruce said, still staring at the pin. "Kent knows a guy who's a jeweler, and he could tell you what it's worth."

"I think she wants to keep it." Carefully David wrapped it up in the white paper.

Bruce waved good-bye, and David watched him climb back up to the river trail. Funny how he kept running into Bruce when he thought he was alone. Was Bruce following him for some reason?

He turned back to the river, doubtful now. This idea of looking for twin trees was beginning to seem ridiculous. He kept walking anyway, studying the tree shapes as he went.

All at once he saw a mist of insects doing a curious sort of flitting dance just above the surface of the river. Mayflies! He stared at them with rising excitement.

He'd read about mayflies, how they existed as nymphs in the mud for several years, then emerged to live for one short day. And here they were in front of him, doing their strange mating dance. In a frenzy of blurred motion, the light green creatures were bouncing straight up into the air, floating down, and then rising again on delicate, transparent wings.

Now it was almost over. Already there were dead mayflies lying on the water like limp feathers.

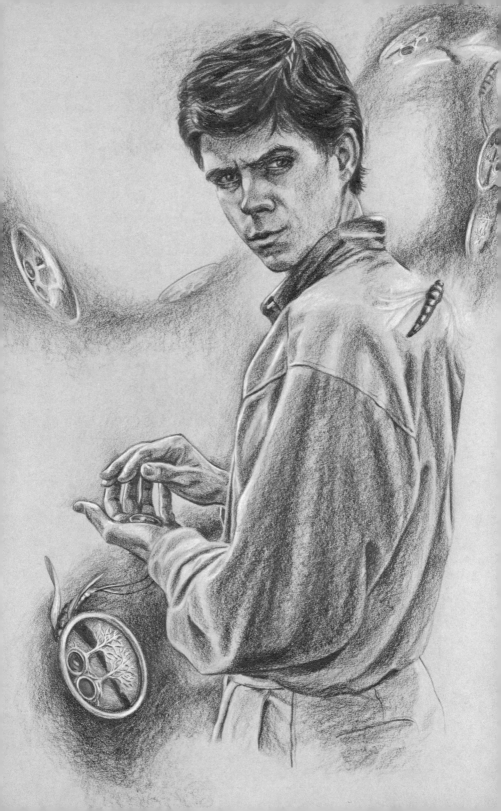

Snatching at the pillboxes in his pocket, he bounded along the rocks that jutted out into the river. He captured several mayflies from a fluttering cloud and scooped up some more from the water. Now he couldn't wait to get to work on his fragile new specimens. It would be a painstaking job to mount and label them properly, but they'd be a great addition to his collection.

When he reached his room, Susan was waiting for him with samples of the cookies she had baked. She stayed to watch while he carefully set the insects to dry, and as soon as he had finished that, she begged him to read her a story. At last she went to bed, and he could enjoy a quiet evening of work.

Automatically he started emptying the pockets of his muddy jeans. He slid a hand into the right front pocket and froze. The moonstone pin . . . where was it? Maybe in the other pocket? No, that was the one with the hole. He'd been especially careful not to put it in there. Hastily he searched his back pockets. He found his tweezers, magnifying glass, paper, pencil—

The pin was gone.

He sat down on his bed with a thump, feeling sick. He was sure he'd put it back after looking at it by the river, because the pillboxes had been in the same pocket, and he'd taken them out to get the pin back in. The pillboxes! When he'd pulled them out to catch the mayflies, the pin must have fallen out too.

In the next minute he was tiptoeing down the stairs and out the back door. He was deep in the woods before he realized how dark it had become. His steps slowed. He couldn't go back and get the flashlight—it was in Susan's room and she would be sure to ask a million questions. What about getting one from the tool shed?

Just then he saw Nannette on the path ahead. When she invited him to visit her, he hesitated, but only for a minute. He couldn't tell her that he'd lost the moonstone pin and had to go look for it. Anyway, he'd have a better chance of finding it in the morning.

Nannette's bright eyes twinkled up at him. "Tonight, for a Sunday evening treat, I will make you some cocoa," she said. "Perhaps, to a young man, that tastes better than chamomile tea, yes?"

"I like anything you make, Nannette," he declared, as they turned down the path to her cottage. He found it easy to tell her about the mayflies and about his idea of looking for the twin trees. But he was glad that she did not ask to see the moonstone pin.

Inside her cottage, a yellow lamp cast a cozy pool of light over the small kitchen table. As soon as David sat down, the cat emerged from the shadows and jumped into his lap.

"Mimi, you're looking fine!" he exclaimed. "You must be better."

"She's going to be all right," Nannette said, measuring sugar, cocoa, and milk into a pan. "She'll be back to visit you any day now. It is wonderful how fast she's healing."

Nannette sat down across from David, and he felt her keen eyes studying him. "How is it between you and your grandfather?"

"I'm not sure." He answered as honestly as he could. "Sometimes I can't help sort of liking him, but mostly it makes me mad when I think about the way he treated Dad. Does Grandfather have something against God?"

"Yes, he does," she said gravely. "His wife died giving birth to your father. I think he always blamed God for that, as if He had deliberately taken her away from him. Then, when your father decided to be a missionary, Philippe felt that God was taking his son away too."

She got up to stir the cocoa and looked thoughtfully at David. "The day is coming when he will understand that we must not get angry at God for these things that seem so cruel in life. Even for the painful things, there is a reason. Someday your grandfather will be convinced of God's love."

David fidgeted in his chair. He wasn't so sure about God's love himself.

Nannette poured hot, frothing cocoa into their cups and handed him a stick of curled brown cinnamon bark to stir with. "You are unhappy again, aren't you?" she said softly. "Tell me, have you ever accepted the Lord Jesus Christ as your Saviour?"

"Well, yes, back when I was six years old," he mumbled. He kept his eyes fixed on his cup, stirring the cocoa until it formed a small brown whirlpool around the cinnamon stick. "One night I was outside looking at the stars, and I suddenly realized that I could never go to heaven because of my sins. So I talked to my mother about it."

He licked at the cinnamon-bark stick while Nannette waited silently. "Mother showed me some verses in the Bible and told me that Jesus had died to take the punishment for my sins. So I asked Him to be my Saviour."

"Do you think you understood what you were doing?"

"I'm pretty sure I did." Then he had to add the truth. "But that was so long ago—sometimes I wonder if I'm a Christian at all anymore."

Nannette smiled at him reassuringly. "God keeps His promises, no matter how you feel about it."

David sipped his cocoa, avoiding her gaze.

"Still, you are not happy, even though you are part of God's family?" she went on relentlessly.

He shrugged. "I don't know. I guess it's important to believe in Jesus for salvation, but the rest of it just doesn't seem real—I mean about God caring for us and all that stuff."

In the silence that followed, he pretended to be busy picking a burr out of Mimi's fluffy tail, and he wished he had stayed in his room.

"How long is it since you've seen your father?" she said at last.

"About five years," he answered, glad that she had changed the subject. "But this time he's coming home to stay."

"I suppose you feel as if you hardly know him anymore?"

"No, it's not too bad, because he writes a lot of letters. He's a really good writer, and he makes it sound as if we're right there with him."

"What do you think would have happened by now if you had not read his letters for the last five years?"

"I guess I'd forget about him some," David said uneasily.

"That's right." Gently she asked, "Do you ever read God's letter to you—the Bible? Perhaps you've learned a lot of facts about Him, but He'll never be real to you unless you read His Word."

The low, rich voice had such intensity that he could not close his ears to it. "David, get to know the Lord Jesus, and you'll find out that He's a wonderful friend."

"How do you know that Jesus can really be a friend?" he asked huskily.

"I know, because He's my friend too. I was just talking to Him a few minutes ago, before I met you on the path."

David's throat tightened until he could not speak. What would it be like to have a friend like that?

He bent his head to watch the cat in his lap, and he felt her cool, wet nose nuzzle his chin. Then she leapt to the floor and disappeared into the darkness.

He got to his feet too and attempted a polite smile for Nannette. "Thank you for the cocoa," he said. "Aunt Jeanne will be wondering where I am. I'd better go now."

She smiled back at him, a warm, understanding smile. But he had an uncomfortable feeling that even while she walked with him down the path, she was talking to that friend of hers again. Talking about *him*.

Chapter Thirteen
Fear

When David finally fell asleep that night, it was only to dream of twisted trees that clutched at him wildly and held him in their choking grasp. He awoke with the sheet in a knot around his neck. After he had tucked it in again, he drank a glass of water and went back to bed.

While he was drifting off to sleep, a soft murmur of words whispered through his mind: *I have loved thee with an everlasting love. . . .* He recognized it as one of the Bible verses he'd learned for the contest, and he tried not to listen. But the tender words pattered on endlessly: *I have loved thee. . . . I have loved thee with an everlasting love. . . . I have loved thee. . . .* At last he slept.

The chime of a clock startled him awake, and he sat up to look out his window. It was barely dawn, with fog hanging low in the trees. He glanced at his watch. He could have slept for hours yet. Why did he have this blurred sense that something dreadful had happened?

Then memory came crowding back, and with it came the cold, sick feeling of yesterday. Aunt Jeanne's moonstone pin. He'd promised himself that he'd get up early this morning to find it. Noiselessly he slipped into his clothes, crept down the stairs, and stole out into the soft, gray morning. He hurried through the misty woods, brushing past spider webs that hung like silver veils across the path. At last he reached the river and stumbled down the bank.

How far had he gone yesterday? These were the rocks that jutted out into the river. This had to be the place. He remembered standing right on this spot when he pulled the pillboxes out of his pocket. But where was the pin?

Kneeling, he sifted frantically through the loose sand. He crawled across all the rocks, looking for a glint of reflected light or a fluttering piece of white paper.

Nothing.

What was he going to tell Aunt Jeanne?

He slumped onto the sand and stared miserably at the long drifts of mist that hovered, thick and pale, over the dark river. He'd wanted to be a peacemaker, like Aunt Lucy had said. He'd wanted to find the pistols so that Dad could come home, but he'd only messed things up. Now he was all alone in this tangle. What was he going to do?

For the first time in a long while, he felt the sting of tears behind his eyelids. "Think!" he commanded himself. But his mind only swirled with despair.

Then, softly through the misted silence, he heard it again. *I have loved thee with an everlasting love. . . . I have loved thee. . . .*

God's words. Maybe he wasn't alone. God loved him. Jesus Christ had died for him—he couldn't escape that. *I have loved thee, David, with an everlasting love. . . .*

As he listened, the Word burned into him, sharp and cleansing.

Bowing his head, he whispered, "Thank you, Lord Jesus, for loving me so much, even when I ignored You. I need You to take charge of my life. Please help me now. . . ." He ran out of words and looked up.

Sunrise had crept over the dark line of trees in the east, making the fog glimmer with pearly light. Like the moonstone.

Panic struck. "Lord, I forgot to tell you about the moonstone pin. I lost it."

Slowly a verse materialized in his mind: *Fear thou not; for I am with thee: be not dismayed; for I am thy God.* It was another one of those contest verses, but now it had new meaning. The Lord knew about that pin. And even better, he'd never have to feel alone again. While the sun burned through the fog, dissolving it into radiance, David lingered on the riverbank with peace spreading deep inside him.

He took one last look for the moonstone pin. Maybe now he would find it. But the sandy margin of the river was still empty, with only the young willows there, trembling in the breeze. He turned away and scrambled up the bluff, feeling slightly foolish. He'd half expected the Lord to do a little miracle for him and have that pin just reappear.

Be not dismayed—that meant *trust Him,* didn't it? Trusting wasn't as easy as it sounded, but he'd keep on trying.

As David walked back through the woods, it occurred to him that Kelly might be a big help in looking for the pin. It could be anywhere along here, actually, and she spent more time down at the river than he did.

Absorbed in his thoughts, he passed the hangar and had almost reached the house when he saw Susan skipping down the trail toward him. Behind her strode his grandfather.

"Hi, David," Susan cried. "We're going to look at 55 Charlie. Grandfather says he got too jealous of the other planes, and now he's turned green with envy."

David remembered that Bruce had sprayed the airplane with green primer last night. He laughed, joining in her huge enjoyment of the joke.

His sister grabbed his hand. "Come on with us," she urged. "I want to see how it looks."

David let her tug him toward the hangar. Until he found that pin, he wanted to stay away from Aunt Jeanne anyway.

In the hangar, Susan wrinkled up her nose. "Smells like someone's been painting, that's for sure. Oh, 55 Charlie, you look funny!"

She was right, David decided, surveying the drab green plane. Its paper-covered windshield gave it the odd appearance of being blindfolded.

"Looks really good," Grandfather remarked to Bruce and Kent, who were lounging against the workbench.

Bruce nodded. "Thanks." He glanced at David, his gray eyes remote. "You going to be around to help us sand it this afternoon?"

"Sure," David said. "That sounds like a big job."

"It is," Bruce answered glumly. He walked to the hangar door with David's grandfather. "Do you know where my dad is?" he asked.

"Yes, he's up at the house talking to Jeanne and probably eating some of her coffee cake," answered Grandfather. "Why don't you go on up and join him?"

"Nah, I'll just stick around here," replied Bruce. "Hey, did you see the new automatic pilot he put in his plane?"

"Yes," said Grandfather. "He was telling me about it. Come and take a look, Dave." He walked over to Mr. Jonson's bronze-striped airplane and opened the cockpit door. As David bent to look at the instrument panel, his grandfather threw him an inquiring glance. "I'm going to take the plane up and try it out. Why don't you come with me?"

The hairs prickled up on David's neck, and he jerked out of the cockpit.

"Oh, can I come?" asked Susan.

His quick hope that she might go instead was dashed when his grandfather answered, "No, the back seat is out right now, and you went last time. I think it's only fair for Dave to have a turn."

As David hesitated, he heard Kent's voice beside him, low and scornful. "What's the matter, you scared of heights?"

Grandfather went on briskly, "Go ahead and hop in, Dave, and I'll do the preflight."

He stumbled around the tail of the plane, his dragging feet catching in the tufts of rough grass. No way to get out of it now.

He could feel the old fear squeezing at him, and he fought back. Relentlessly it tightened until he was choking with panic, gasping for breath.

"Help, Lord!" he cried silently as Kent's blond head appeared behind him.

Fear thou not, for I am with thee. . . . The verse flowed into his mind, cool and swift as a rush of river water. The panic disappeared, and he could breathe again. He filled his lungs with air and wrenched the cabin door open, ignoring Kent's contemptuous grin.

His grandfather turned on the key, and the propeller spun into a blur. David fumbled with his seat belt, finally pulling it tight as they bumped over the grass. At the end of the runway, Grandfather slowed the plane and checked the instruments and controls.

While his grandfather completed the preflight check, David allowed his mind to wander, and he became aware of a cold inner voice: "The last time you were in a little plane like this, it crashed on takeoff, didn't it?" He shivered as he listened, and his fear began to grow again.

All at once the airplane was moving forward, bouncing over the turf and gathering speed, faster and faster. He wanted to cry out, but his voice was caught somewhere inside him, lost in the frantic pounding of his heart. He turned his head, pretending to look out the window.

As the plane sprang into the air, David closed his eyes and gritted his teeth. He struggled to concentrate on the promise he had been given: *Fear thou not; for I am with thee. . . . Fear thou not. . . .* Suddenly his eyes were open and the plane was flying smoothly, with the wonderful resonant hum that he remembered.

Far below, he could see the orange windsock on the dark-roofed barn, smooth green pastures, and fuzzy-looking trees fringing the silver expanse of the river.

Before long, his grandfather engaged the autopilot. "We'll use St. Louis VOR," he said. "Then we pick a course. Now I'll put it into the navigational mode."

David watched, fascinated, as the plane gently turned toward the proper heading. His grandfather remarked, "Yes, I can see why Bob's so proud of his new autopilot. It really works better than the old one."

A few minutes later he asked David, "Here, do you want to try flying it? I'll punch the autopilot off. Just relax and try to keep the wings level with this." He tapped the control wheel.

David took the wheel into his hands gingerly, but it wasn't long before he was enjoying himself. He had forgotten how much fun it was to fly.

"You handle that pretty well," said his grandfather, looking pleased.

"My father used to take me flying with him," David said. "He let me try it a couple of times. He's a very good pilot," he added defensively.

"He should be," Grandfather's voice was gruff. "I taught him to fly myself. He was the best student I ever had, even better than Bruce."

"I didn't know you taught Bruce to fly," said David. "Isn't his father an instructor too?"

"Yes, he is, but they don't get along very well sometimes. I felt sorry for the boy. He wanted to learn, but Bob never let him develop any confidence in himself." His grandfather looked at his watch. "I guess we'd better head back to the field."

His experienced hands moved over the controls, and soon they were coming in low over the line of trees, toward the grass runway in the pasture. They dropped down swiftly until David felt the main wheels touch, and then they were bumping over the grass again on their way to the hangar.

After turning off the engine, Grandfather said in a quiet voice, "The other day, I thought you were just being polite, letting Susan and your aunt go up in the plane."

David could not meet his eyes. He stared straight ahead, out of the cockpit window.

His grandfather went on gravely. "You said you used to fly with your father. Did something happen?"

David cleared his throat. "A while ago, I was in a plane that crashed. It was a small plane like this one. Susan was injured and my mother was killed. That's why we had to come and live in the States." Out of the corner of his eye, he saw a shadow cross his grandfather's face.

Impulsively he added, "I've been afraid of flying ever since. But this morning, I got something straightened out with God, and—well—He helped me through it."

His grandfather's mouth tightened into a grim line, and David knew that the moment of closeness was gone. But all Grandfather said was, "I'm sorry about your mother. Do you feel better about flying now?"

"Yes," answered David simply. And in his heart he knew it was true. The old fear had lost its power. For a minute he wondered what would happen the next time he got into an airplane, then he brushed the thought aside.

Chapter Fourteen
Kelly's Secret

After lunch, David slipped up to his room and shut the door, hoping that Susan would take a hint and stay away. He dug his Bible out of his suitcase, and after looking up the word "fear" in the concordance at the back, he found the verse that had been on his mind all morning: Isaiah 41:10.

He read it over several times and then closed his Bible slowly. The moonstone pin and the pistols still were missing, but now he felt differently about the whole problem. *Be not dismayed,* the Lord had said. Okay, he'd keep on trusting.

As he put his Bible into the desk drawer, a green card fell to the floor. It was a Bible-reading schedule from Sunday school that he'd stuck in his Bible and forgotten. He picked up the small card and studied it. Nannette seemed to think that reading the Bible was important if he was really going to know Christ. This might be a good way to get started; he'd begin tonight.

Right now, though, he had to find Kelly and tell her what had happened to him. She was probably down at the river. He picked up a collecting jar to take with him in case he found anything interesting, and then he opened the door.

Susan appeared immediately, and he knew she had been waiting for him to come out. "Oh, please," she said, when she saw the jar in his hand. "Can I come?"

"I'm just going down to the river," he said. "Come along if you want to." That was the trouble with having a kid sister; he'd rather have talked to Kelly alone.

When they first reached the river, David made another careful search of the rocks where he'd caught the mayflies, without telling Susan what he was looking for. He didn't want her blabbing to Aunt Jeanne about how he'd lost the pin. Especially since he still couldn't find it. He turned upstream, trying not to feel discouraged.

"Oh, look, Mimi's following us," called Susan. He saw a gray plume whisking through the bushes, and he had to grin when his sister ran off to catch the cat.

All the way to the summerhouse, he kept his eyes open for twisted trees while he looked for Kelly. When he reached the bluff where the summerhouse stood, he skidded hopefully down a steep path that led to the river's edge. He knew that Kelly often came here, but today the sandy strip was deserted.

He sat on a weathered log that was part of a jumble of uprooted trees that sprawled across the sand and into the river. Hearing a giggle behind him, he turned and saw Susan sliding down the path with her arms full of the squirming gray cat. "Better put her down," he called. "Cats don't like—"

Before he could finish, Mimi leaped from Susan's arms and landed with a thump on the sand. Flinging a disgruntled look over her shoulder, the cat sprang lightly onto a tree limb beside David and scampered along its length to where the dead branches hung into the river. There she crouched, staring intently at something in the water.

Intrigued, he followed her and discovered that she was watching a swirling mass of glittering black beetles. "Susan," he called, "come and look at the whirligig beetles."

She came running, and perched beside him on the fallen tree. "They're cute, like little black submarines. How come they don't sink?"

"Surface tension," he said. "I wish we had a fly. You ought to see the way they attack their food."

"Are you going to get some for your collection?"

"I sure am. Here, hold this top, would you?" He dipped up a few of the beetles and closed the collecting jar. "Let's get back to the house. I want to see if I've got any good specimens."

Susan laughed. "At least you know where to get lots more if you need them. There goes that cat! I'm going to catch her for sure this time. Oh, here's Kelly." She waved at Kelly, who was coming down the bank toward them, and then dashed away after the cat.

"Hi, Kelly," David said, crossing the sand to meet her. "I've got some whirligigs for my collection. We've been watching them, and they're the craziest—" He broke off in embarrassment, remembering how he had walked away from her the day before.

He tried again. "Hey, about yesterday, I want to tell you—"

But she was holding something out to him, with an uneasy look that just grazed the top of his head and did not meet his eyes. "Here—my brother—he found this."

She thrust a small object at him and ran up the slope into the trees before he could say anything.

He looked down at his hand and felt like shouting. She had given him the moonstone pin.

"How in the world?" He stared into the woods where she had gone, his happiness mingled with puzzlement at her behavior.

Finally he picked up his jar and climbed back up to the trail. "Susan," he called. "Come on, let's go."

"I'm coming," answered a faint voice.

As David stood waiting for her, he glanced back at the beach below him, at the tree limbs where he had been sitting.

It looked like two trees, actually, joined at the roots, with twin trunks. . . .

Eagerly he studied the tangled mass. Could that be Aunt Jeanne's tree? It might have been growing right here at the edge of the river, twenty years ago. Maybe it fell over when the river washed away the bank. Obviously the pistols weren't in the tree, but perhaps she had hidden them somewhere nearby.

The woods behind him sloped up into a small hill that was studded with rocky outcroppings. There might be a cave behind one of those ledges.

He had already started toward the hill when he remembered that he still held Aunt Jeanne's brooch. "First take it back to her," he told himself grimly. Later this afternoon he would do the exploring. He slid his hand into his pocket as Susan skipped down the path toward him, panting and disheveled.

"Did you catch Mimi?" he asked.

"Yup," she answered triumphantly. "But then I let her go."

As soon as David got back to his room, he placed the moonstone pin carefully in its brown leather box. Snatching up a pencil, he made a quick sketch of the pin, wondering if he'd been mistaken about the fallen tree by the river.

He took one last look and snapped the box closed. Would he ever figure it out in time? Here it was Monday already, and he was no nearer to finding the pistols than he'd been when his father's letter arrived on Friday.

He had to admit that he was beginning to dread the thought of leaving this river valley. The river itself had worked its charm on him: one day it was a gentle green swish of water, and the next, a foaming, boiling, brown torrent. Its banks were fragrant with the scent of growing things, alive with birds, small creatures, and insects . . . and it was his father's country.

A defeated feeling crept over him, and he tried to shake it off. " 'Be not dismayed. . . .' " This time he said the verse aloud. " 'For I am thy God.' "

Dismayed. That reminded him of the expression he'd seen on Kelly's face. She hadn't acted as if she were mad at him. It almost seemed that she was scared about something. He'd have to tell her about the verse.

He picked up the moonstone pin and went to look for Aunt Jeanne. He found her in the kitchen, and when he handed her the jeweler's box, she dropped it into her apron pocket without opening it. "Are you still looking for the pistols?" she asked, keeping her eyes on the carrots she was peeling.

"Yes," David said. "I have another idea that I want to check. Were the guns stored in a wooden case?"

"Of course. It was a beautiful, polished mahogany case, lined with red velvet." She sighed. "Dave, you know that it is impossible after all these years."

"I don't care," he answered. "They've got to be around here somewhere. I know my father didn't take them."

Suddenly he realized that Grandfather was standing in the doorway, his mouth tight and unsmiling. He must have overheard. David stiffened, expecting an angry comment.

But the old man only turned and walked into the library, shutting the door.

Aunt Jeanne's voice was soft. "Sometimes I think he is sorry for the foolish pride that has kept him so bitter for all these years." She shook her head sadly. "He is stubborn, just as you are."

After he left Aunt Jeanne, David remembered his promise to help Bruce and trotted down the path toward the hangar. If he hurried, maybe he could get some work done on the airplane and still have time to go back to the river before supper.

When he reached the hangar, he found Bruce leaning against the workbench, staring into space. He grinned at David in a curiously vague way and mumbled, "Well, I guess we'd better get busy and sand this old crate, huh?" After fumbling around on the workbench, he found two sheets of black sandpaper and handed one to David.

"You take that side and I'll do this one," he said, stepping to the left side of the airplane. "Just sand it lightly enough to take off the gloss. If you do it too hard, it's no good." He wiped a sleeve across his red, watery eyes. "Watch out for the rivet heads."

David went to work, sanding the door smoothly and carefully. But when he reached the rear window, he sanded all the primer off the heads of three rivets before he realized what had happened. Instead of being green, they now gleamed the dull silver of bare metal.

He was going to ask what to do about it when Bruce started telling him how he'd learned to fly and how much he admired David's grandfather. "He's a good pilot, and he really knows how to handle a plane. Someday, I'm going to be as good as him, you know that?" Bruce took a swipe at the airplane with his sandpaper. "And someday, I'm going to be rich like him, and live in a big house too."

David thought of the cracked plaster and faded rugs in the old house, but didn't say anything. He stopped working long enough to open the window beside him. The paint fumes in the hangar seemed to be sickeningly sweet today. The odor reminded him of something else, but he couldn't remember exactly what it was.

"Money," Bruce was saying. "That's the thing. And not someday, either. Right now. I'd like to have loads of money— I sure could use it." He lapsed into dreamy silence for a few minutes.

Finally he said, "I've had it with this job. I'm going to take off for a while. Promised Kent I'd meet him." He peered over at David's work. "Looks good. Why don't you go ahead and finish that side, and we'll do some more tomorrow."

"Okay," David agreed, and picked up a fresh sheet of sandpaper. After Bruce left, he gazed regretfully at the long, slanting side of the airplane. There was a lot more to sand— he'd never have time to get down to the river before supper. Since it got dark so fast in the woods, he might as well wait until tomorrow to explore that hillside.

After supper, David busied himself with setting up his insect traps, using the cloth strips and the sweet fermented mixture Aunt Jeanne had been saving for him. Susan helped him carry his supplies and a lantern out to a pasture beside the house, where he tacked the strips to several fence posts. Next he smeared the brown, sticky mixture over the white fabric.

"Ugh," Susan said. "That stuff looks awful."

"To you, perhaps," he answered. "But to an insect, it's just like dessert. You wait and see." He turned on the lantern and adjusted it so that the light fell on the widest of the strips. "This one with the light shining on it will have more visitors, I think. We'll come back later and find out what we've caught."

He headed toward his room to fold some small paper envelopes for carrying any moths they might catch.

Before long, dusk had deepened to darkness, and Susan began asking him when they were going to check the insect traps. He let her carry the flashlight, and together they walked through the pasture toward the white strips.

His sister tramped silently beside him instead of chattering as he'd expected. Concerned, he glanced at her drooping figure. Even in the dim light he could see the unhappiness on her face, and it perplexed him.

When they reached the traps, she watched without saying anything while he shook several fluttering insects off the sticky sheet and into his jar.

Finally he asked, "What's the matter, kid?"

She shrugged. "I guess it's nothing, really."

"C'mon, tell me," he urged, snatching at a June bug that zoomed out of the jar to freedom.

"It's just that—I miss Daddy," she said in a low voice. "Sometimes I wonder if you'll ever be able to find those pistols, or if we'll have to go away from here to some strange place—and somewhere else might be awful—and then maybe Daddy won't be able to get well. . . ." Her voice trembled, and she wiped her eyes, leaving long, grimy smears down her cheeks.

David capped the jar and set it down so he could put an arm around her shoulders. It was so unlike her to be crying that he hardly knew what to say.

"Yeah, it's scary," he admitted. He remembered his newfound friend with a rush of gratitude and added, "But the Lord is taking care of us. He even gave me a special promise." David quoted the verse from Isaiah for her and then gave her a quick hug. "I miss Dad too."

She sniffed a few times and lifted her head to watch a tall figure coming across the pasture. "Oh, there's Grandfather."

"Your aunt is afraid that you're being eaten alive by mosquitoes out here," Grandfather said when he reached them. He shone his flashlight toward one of the sticky strips. "It looks as if your trap is working fine."

"Yes, it's going to take me a while to mount these critters and find out what they are," David said.

He let go of Susan to pick up another jar. His grandfather must have heard her still sniffling, for he flicked his light over her tear-stained face. "Susan, are you all right?"

She nodded, blinking in the glare of the flashlight, but his question hung heavily, unanswered.

"Did you get hurt?" Grandfather persisted.

David flipped a velvety gray moth off the sheet and slipped it into one of his envelopes. "She's worried about Dad," he said in a tight voice.

There was a small, awkward silence, and he could hear the crickets chirping madly in the next pasture. Then his grandfather held out a hand to the little girl and his deep voice was unexpectedly gentle. "It's getting late, Susan; why don't you come in now? Aunt Jeanne said that you like stories. Would you like me to read you one?"

Susan went willingly, and David was left alone in the dark pasture. After collecting the rest of the insects, he stacked up his jars. He switched off the lantern, and the star-pricked sky above him sprang into view. As he hunted for his favorite constellation, Leo the Lion, he was filled with awe. How great, how powerful, was this God who had promised to be with him! It was wonderful to have such a friend.

On his way back across the shadowy grass, he saw that the hangar was lighted. Bruce must have come back to do some more sanding on the airplane. Then a light blinked on upstairs in the old house. That would be Grandfather's studio. Maybe he was reading Susan her story in there, surrounded by paintings.

It was a nice thing for him to do, David conceded. But after all, it was his grandfather's stubborn bitterness that caused her unhappiness in the first place. He searched for the anger that usually came boiling up when he thought about his grandfather, but it seemed to have faded. Suddenly David found himself praying for Grandfather. If only he knew Jesus Christ, everything would be different.

Chapter Fifteen
Bruce

The next morning, David was glad to see that Susan was her usual bright self again. She skipped into his room before breakfast, full of plans for the day. Nannette had invited her to come for lunch, and Aunt Jeanne had promised that they would bake some special cookies to take along. "I had a nice visit with Grandfather," she added. "We had a long talk, all about Daddy."

She sniffed the air like a puppy. "Can you smell bacon? Hurry up!" She clattered away, leaving David to wonder what Grandfather had told her.

"She could charm anyone," he told himself consolingly, and he clumped down the stairs for breakfast.

During the meal, his grandfather asked about the insects David had collected and offered to help him with the job of identifying them. David found himself thinking that Grandfather seemed friendlier than he used to be, and his happiness at the discovery took him by surprise.

They walked down to the hangar together and found Bruce sanding the nose of the airplane. He looked better today, although he didn't have a smile for either of them.

"Look at that side you sanded yesterday," he snapped at David. "What did you use, a power sander?"

"I was going to ask you about the rivets," David began.

"Rivets!" exclaimed Bruce. "Never mind the rivets. Look at that door."

Bewildered, David stepped toward the right side of the airplane, where he had worked yesterday. But Bruce shouldered past him. "Over here. This is where you were sanding, and if I'd known you couldn't even do this much by yourself, I wouldn't have taken off."

David followed him to the left side, aware that Kent was slouched against the tail of the airplane, watching. He stared at the door where Bruce had worked yesterday. The bare metal was showing through the green primer in long, ugly streaks.

He shot a glance of amazement at Bruce. "But I—"

"Never mind," retorted Bruce. "There's nothing you can do about it now. The rest of it doesn't look too bad. I'll spray it again and touch up the rivets, and it'll be okay." He turned away. "But next time, pay attention to what you're doing."

Conscious of his grandfather's keen gaze upon him, David took a step after Bruce. "Hey, wait a minute—" he began. But Bruce had flipped on the compressor that powered the spray gun. Its busy *putt-putt-putt* filled the hangar and drowned out David's voice.

He bit his lip and walked over to the other side of the airplane. Yes. There were the three rivets he'd sanded too hard. He even remembered opening the window over here. Had Bruce messed up his side of the plane and then conveniently blamed it on him?

He had to explain to Grandfather what had really happened. But now he was busy helping Kent at the workbench. Besides, David thought with a pang, Grandfather would probably believe Bruce's story anyway.

With a last glance towards the workbench he turned to go, but something about the back of Kent's head made him take another look. He paused. From this angle, Kent sure did look like the blond boy who had stood beside the silver-haired lady at the airport. That kid had disappeared at just about the same time her jewelry had been stolen, he remembered. But what did that prove?

He dismissed the idea as he left the hangar, thinking that if he went down to the river he might find Kelly. His steps quickened. With everything that had happened, he had a lot to tell her.

The river seemed deserted, however, so he had to be content with doing the exploration he'd planned. He tramped up and down the hill behind the little stone house, examining every ledge and outcropping of rock, but there wasn't a hint of anything hidden there.

That afternoon he went back again, telling himself that he hadn't searched the stone house thoroughly, but he found only two abandoned wasps' nests up near the roof. And there was still no sign of Kelly.

By the next morning he was beginning to feel desperate. Today was Wednesday. Mr. Jonson had made all the arrangements for their airline tickets, and tomorrow was their last day here.

The only good thing that had happened was his new closeness to God. The chapters he'd been reading in the Gospel of John told about Christ's power over the forces of evil, and the more David read, the more he found Him to be a fascinating person.

He sat down at his desk and gazed at the insects he still had to write up for his report. For once he didn't feel like working on them. He'd take a walk along the river. . . . Kelly might be there.

Maybe she'd been sick yesterday. Or worse, maybe she had decided to stay away from him. "Here you are, stewing with worries again," he scolded himself. "Some trusting Christian you are."

"What did you say?" Susan poked her head in the door.

"I was just talking to myself," David mumbled.

"Yes, but what were you saying?"

He sighed. "I told myself to shut up and trust God, like He wants me to."

For a moment she looked puzzled, but then she smiled. "Are you going to?" Without waiting for an answer, she added, "Tell Kelly 'hi' for me if you find her." She tossed back her blond hair and disappeared.

As David strolled past the hangar, he heard someone working there and stopped to watch. Bruce was spraying white paint on the airplane, concentrating hard, and he didn't look up. The noisy compressor made conversation difficult anyway, David reminded himself as he left. He had to admit that lately Bruce had lost his friendly grin. Maybe he felt guilty about blaming David for his carelessness in sanding the airplane.

Kelly wasn't on the rocks below the steep bluff, so David walked upriver toward the summerhouse. As soon as he reached the small clearing he saw her, and his heart leaped. She was bent over her sketchbook, down by the water where he'd caught the whirligig beetles. He bounded down the steep path.

Hurriedly Kelly stood up, dropping her pencil in the sand. As she leaned over to pick it up, her blue sweater slipped off one shoulder. She snatched it back into place over her blouse, but not before David had seen two large bruises on her upper arm.

"Hi," he said, trying to sound casual. "Seen any interesting barbules lately?"

She answered with a faint smile. It was so unlike her usual sparkling grin that he knew something was wrong.

"What happened to your arm?" he asked, coming a step closer. She jerked away from him as if to escape, and the sweater slid off onto the sand.

He couldn't help staring at the livid purple of those bruises. "Who did that to you?" he demanded.

She gave him a despairing look, and he read the answer in her eyes before she turned away.

"Was it Bruce?" He picked up the sweater and stepped around to face her.

She nodded, her eyes lowered.

He saw tears glittering on her dark eyelashes, and his hands tightened on the sweater, clenching into fists. He felt like smashing those fists into Bruce's face.

Kelly glanced up at him. "David, don't look so savage," she protested in a shaky voice. "He didn't mean to hurt me. He was just mad that I took it away from him."

"What did you take away from Bruce?" he asked.

She gave him another anxious glance and sank down onto the fallen tree. After draping the blue sweater around her shoulders, he sat on another limb, facing her.

"It was the moonstone pin," she said. "I saw it in his room. He said he'd found it by the river one evening, and that Kent was going to sell it for him. So I brought it back to you. I've never seen him so angry."

She locked her hands together and stared at them. "It's just because he wants the money so badly—that's all that he and Kent think about. I wish he wouldn't run around with someone like Kent."

"So Kent was going to sell it for him," David said. "It fits."

"What do you mean?"

"I think Kent knows quite a bit about the jewelry business," David answered. He told her what had happened at the airport and about his suspicions of Kent. "I sure hope Bruce isn't part of whatever is going on."

Kelly shook her head miserably. "All I know is that he gets pot from Kent, and the whole bunch of them smoke it. That's why he always needs money. I wish he could get away! We've got some relatives in Pittsburgh who are Christians, but I'm afraid Dad won't let him go."

Then her words rushed out as if she had kept them to herself for too long. "David, he's so awful when he's spaced-out—it's scary. You know the horrible thing that happened to Mimi? I found out that he and Kent did it. They were shooting at her with their slingshots, but she got away from them. It's—it's so bad when he's high on pot, sometimes he doesn't even know what's going on. And there's nothing I can do. . . ." Her voice trailed off hopelessly.

David leaned toward her. "Hey, there *is* something we can do. Let's talk to the Lord about it." She nodded and then slowly bowed her head.

He hadn't planned what to say, but for once the words came smoothly as he asked God to work in Bruce's heart.

When he finished praying, Kelly lifted her head, and he saw that her blue eyes were shining again. "You're different today," she said softly. "What happened?"

"I found out that God really does care," David answered simply. "And I asked Him to take control of my life. I learned a verse—you'll like it—'Fear thou not; for I am with thee: be not dismayed; for I am thy God.' "

"Be not dismayed," she repeated. "That's for me, all right."

"Hey, Kelly!" It was Susan's voice, shrilling through the trees.

David grinned at her ruefully. "Kid sisters!"

"Kelly?" Susan peered down from the bluff over their heads. "Nannette sent me to remind you about your painting lesson."

"Coming right now," Kelly called. She flashed a quick smile at David and scrambled up the slope.

He watched her go, wishing he'd had time to tell her about the twin trees. Susan joined him a minute later.

"Don't you think this looks like two trees?" he asked her, pointing to the tree limbs where they were sitting.

She cocked her head to study the uprooted trees. "I guess so. And the roots are all grown together. They're awfully old, aren't they?"

"Yes," he said absently, his eyes half-closed. He was trying to imagine what it must have been like on that stormy night, long ago. Aunt Jeanne had probably come running down here. The blowing rain would have drenched her, since she wasn't wearing a raincoat—or was she? Terrified, she had headed for her favorite tree, looking for a place to hide the guns. Why hadn't she—

Something buzzed past him and landed with a plop in the water. He heard another soft hiss and ducked instinctively.

"David!" cried Susan. "Someone's shooting at us!"

Chapter Sixteen
The Hide-out

David caught a flicker of movement in the trees behind the summerhouse as another silent missile grazed his cheek.

He grabbed for Susan, dragged her down off the log, and plunged toward the overhanging bank. There they pressed themselves close against the roots that twined out of the sandy earth.

He held his breath, listening. The river dimpled as more shots hit the water and sank. Two, three, four. Susan huddled closer to him.

Suddenly the shooting stopped. David waited, still tense, aware that the surrounding woods were unnaturally quiet. Even the birds had stopped singing.

Susan whispered in his ear, "Do you think it's Kent with his slingshot?"

He rubbed at the tender spot on his cheek. "Where'd you get that idea?"

"I just have a feeling. I saw him using it to shoot at a squirrel, and his bullets don't make any noise either." She shuddered. "He acted like he was doing it just for the fun of scaring the squirrel to death."

Right away David remembered what Kelly had said about Kent. But this was more than a prank.

He saw the worry on his sister's face and whispered, "We'd better stay quiet for a few minutes. I'm going to ask the Lord what to do."

After a silent prayer, he opened his eyes to find her staring at him expectantly.

"What did He say?" she whispered.

"Wait." The word was there in David's mind, and he knew it was the answer.

She nodded in agreement.

They'd better be hidden from anyone using the path to get down to the river, he decided. One slow step at a time, he crept around the curved side of the bluff, leading Susan. Now his head was almost level with the base of the stone wall that bordered the courtyard of the summerhouse. This would be a good place to wait. Just above him stood one of the three pillars that were part of the wall, and he examined the old stones with interest.

"Look," he whispered to Susan. He pointed to a column of ants streaming in and out of a hole at the bottom of the stone pillar. She edged closer, pulling herself up by the thick vine that grew over the wall.

As she did so, something skittered away on tiny white feet, giving them a glimpse of large glistening eyes and silken gray fur.

"What was that?"

"Looked like a wood rat," David said, almost forgetting to whisper. He pointed to the hole in the pillar that the ants were using. "He probably lives in there, and we woke him up from his nap."

By now he could hear the birds singing again. "Let's go," he said to Susan. "Come on up this way."

They pulled themselves up the slope, clinging to vines and using the gnarled roots of the old willow tree for footholds.

When they reached the stone house, David glanced over his shoulder at the wooded hill above them. That was probably where Kent or whoever-it-was had stood, giving him a perfect view of the river's edge. If Kent had a slingshot as powerful as Bruce's, he could easily shoot that far. Was this supposed to be some kind of warning?

He hurried his sister along the narrow path, using it as a short cut to the main trail. "Susan," he said urgently as they passed the hangar, "don't say anything about this for a while, will you?"

She looked at him. "Why not?"

"I'm trying to figure something out," he said, frowning in concentration. "I want to ask Bruce about Kent before we get the grown-ups involved."

Somehow he had to find out if he was right about Kent and the jewelry thefts. For Kelly's sake, he didn't want to get Bruce in trouble if he could help it. Maybe Bruce didn't even know what Kent was up to.

Aunt Jeanne had lunch ready by the time they arrived at the house. Grandfather was not there, so she and Susan spent most of the meal talking about Nannette. David, only half-listening, was absorbed in thinking about Kelly and her anxiety over Bruce.

Now he realized why the smell that had bothered him in the hangar was familiar. He'd known some kids at school who smoked marijuana, and it was the same sickly sweet odor that had clung to their clothes. Maybe Bruce had still been spaced-out that night when he came back and tried to sand the airplane.

David heard Susan telling Aunt Jeanne about the wood rat, and his mind snapped to attention. There was something about the wood rat and the stone pillar that he'd wondered about and then forgotten . . . some connection that seemed to be important.

All through the rest of the meal, and even afterwards while he was reading a story to Susan, he puzzled over it.

At last he finished the story, and Susan stretched out contentedly on her bed with another book to read by herself. "I'll never forget that little gray mouse we saw," she remarked. "It was the cutest thing."

"Wood rat," he corrected her automatically.

At once the elusive idea clicked into place. A wood rat had found room in the stone pillar for a nest, right? Maybe there was more space inside—enough space for a small gun case.

He had to find out.

"See you later, Susan," he said, holding back his eagerness until he was safely out of her room.

He flung himself down the stairs, out the back door, along the path. When he reached the hangar, he made a quick detour in case Bruce was there. He couldn't miss a chance to talk to him about Kent.

The hangar was so quiet that David could hear the sparrows twittering in the eaves. He saw the finished airplane, gleaming white with its new coat of paint, but no sign of Bruce. He ran on.

Halfway to the river, he began wondering if Kent might be hanging around somewhere. He wished he'd thought to check the bushes by the hangar where Kent usually parked his motorcycle. No time to stop and go back now. The hope of finding something in that stone pillar was irresistible.

As he approached the summerhouse, he remembered this morning's shooting. Was someone still nearby, watching? Before he left the sheltering trees, he paused to scan the courtyard. But the small clearing drowsed peacefully in the afternoon sunlight, and from the wooded hill he heard a robin caroling.

Reassured, he picked his way across the stones and crouched beside the wood rat's hide-out. After exploring its nest with a stick, he pried off two small flat stones to enlarge the hole, then peered in. There was nothing inside. But there *was* an empty space. Although the pillar itself was not more than three feet high, it was broad, and that shallow space could provide a pretty good spot for hiding something.

He moved to the next pillar, encouraged by what he had discovered. But after thumping and pulling at its stones, he had to admit that this pillar was still firmly cemented together.

Only one pillar left. He eyed it doubtfully. A wild grape vine from below the bluff had twined across its top, and a pair of wiry saplings crowded against its base. Patiently he probed through the vine until he found a small, loose stone near the top of the pillar that he could pull off. It left a hole just big enough for his hand.

Dismissing the thought of snakes, he slipped his hand into the darkness of the pillar, touched something, and jerked his hand out fast. He licked at the bloody scrape across his knuckles, trying to figure out what he had felt down there. It wasn't fur and it wasn't alive. He groped for it again.

It seemed like cloth of some sort, but he couldn't get his arm in quite far enough to reach it—couldn't pull it out. He squinted into the hole. Dark cloth, maybe navy blue.

At the top of the pillar he found a long, flat stone that felt loose. He wrenched at it, but it was held tightly in place by the stubborn vine. With his pocketknife he hacked unsuccessfully at the vine's crisscrossing woody stems. They were so tough that his small knife seemed to bounce right off. He dug at the green trunks of the young trees wedged at the base of the pillar, but they were too deeply rooted to move. Brushing the perspiration out of his eyes, he sat back on his heels, fighting discouragement.

"All I can do is scratch at it, but that's got to be Aunt Jeanne's raincoat," he muttered. Then he thought of the tool shed behind the rose garden. He could get a saw and cut through that vine in no time.

He plunged at full speed down the short-cut path, slowing to a trot as he reached the main trail. When he neared the house, he saw Aunt Jeanne's face at the kitchen window. A moment later, she appeared on the back porch.

"Oh, here's Dave," she said, sounding relieved. "Philippe, Dave's out here. He can help you carry them down."

Slowly David walked toward the porch steps, conscious of his dirty hands and the perspiration trickling down the sides of his face.

His grandfather stepped out the back door and eyed him with friendly interest. "It looks like you've been digging up an ant colony," he said, and then he smiled.

The smile astonished David. His grandfather had smiled at him! He tried to harden himself against the warmth of that smile—tried and failed.

"You could be a big help to me, if you don't mind," Grandfather was saying. "I have one more load of paintings to take to the showing. Could you help me carry them down to the car?"

"Sure," David said. That wouldn't take long. "I'll be right there." He ran up the stairs two at a time, rinsed off his hands, and followed his grandfather into the studio.

David had never seen a painter's studio before, and if he hadn't been in such a hurry, he would have liked to linger there. As it was, he had a quick impression of canvases stacked against the wall, scattered papers, and tubes of brightly colored paint. Amidst the clutter, brushes stood stiffly upright in their jars.

Gingerly he picked up the painting his grandfather pointed out and carried it downstairs. After they had packed a dozen paintings in the back of the station wagon, his grandfather said, "Thanks very much. How would you like to come along with me for the ride? Have you ever seen an art gallery?"

As David hesitated, he saw a flicker of something resembling disappointment in his grandfather's dark eyes. The pillar would have to wait. "Well, I'm pretty dirty," he said hurriedly. "But I can clean up real fast."

He ran back down the stairs after changing and heard his sister in the kitchen, talking to Aunt Jeanne. For one panic-filled moment, he wished Susan were coming too, so he wouldn't have to make conversation with his grandfather.

But it wasn't as hard to do as he'd thought. While they drove along the country road, his grandfather began talking about his paintings and how he'd started by drawing insects that he'd collected, just as David liked to do. Before he knew it, David was telling him about his science teacher and then about his life with Aunt Lucy.

When David shyly mentioned the letter Nannette had written him, Grandfather chuckled deep in his throat. "That Nannette is still a firebrand, even at her age. When the letter came from your Aunt Lucy, I didn't really know what to do about it. Nannette gave me the worst scolding I've had since I was ten years old. She snatched it up and marched off to answer it herself."

He glanced at David, sobering. "The next thing I knew, you two were here. I'm sorry you kids have had such a rough time."

"It hasn't been that bad," David said. Cautiously he added, "I'm beginning to learn about trusting God with my life. I know He has a plan for it."

His grandfather interrupted, his voice harsh. "You're telling me that all the problems you've had are part of God's plan for your life?"

"There's a verse that says 'All things work together for good to them that love God,' " David said, remembering his father's favorite verse. Now it made sense to him. "I think it means that nothing happens unless He allows it to."

His grandfather grunted, "What about those who don't love God?"

"Well, I guess they have to get along without Him somehow," David said hesitantly. "When I tried it, I was pretty miserable."

"You're beginning to sound like your father," Grandfather answered. But his voice didn't have its usual gruff undertone, and a few minutes later they were talking comfortably about the insects David had added to his collection.

When they reached the gallery where the art show was to take place, David quickly unloaded the paintings into a storage room. He was glad to see his grandfather get back into the car right away, saying that he would return tomorrow to hang them.

As they pulled out of their parking space, a blue police car turned off the highway and stopped behind them. The driver waved at David's grandfather. "Hi, Philip, how's it going?"

David recognized the gray-haired policeman who had questioned him at the airport. He slouched low in his seat, hoping the man wouldn't notice that he was there.

"Just fine," Grandfather answered, smiling. "Did you ever catch your invisible thief at the airport?"

"Not yet. But we got a new lead today, and we're working on it. I'll let you know how it turns out."

"Thanks, Rick," Grandfather said. "See you later."

They eased into the stream of traffic on the highway, and David sat in tense silence. Finally his grandfather gave him a quick sideways glance. "Don't worry about Rick," he said kindly. "He told me that he knew you were clean, but he had to check you out because the woman made a complaint. Rick's a good friend of mine."

David let out a silent breath of relief. So Grandfather had known all along. It felt good not to have to wonder anymore.

As they drove on, his grandfather told him more about the policeman, and he tried to listen. But all he wanted to do now was get back to the stone house. In a hurry. He could feel himself quivering on the edge of the car seat, like a captured moth on the verge of freedom.

He stole another glance at his watch, thinking about Aunt Jeanne's coat, hidden in the pillar. Had she wrapped it around the gun case? Soon he would know.

His grandfather was telling him that Mr. Jonson planned to fly over to see them this evening, after he'd finished a skydiving session. Silently David hoped that Bruce wouldn't be coming too. He did want to talk to him, but not now.

As soon as Grandfather stopped the car in front of the house, David jumped out. But before he could slip around to the back, he heard Aunt Jeanne's voice from the porch. "Supper is ready, you two," she called.

He threw a despairing glance at the setting sun. He would have to eat quickly.

Chapter Seventeen
Danger in the Dark

Because of Mr. Jonson's visit that evening, Aunt Jeanne hurried the meal along, but it didn't go fast enough for David. Finally the moment came when he could excuse himself.

Aunt Jeanne looked out at the darkening sky, her face worried. "There's going to be a storm, Dave."

"I'll be back soon," he promised.

First he went to the tool shed for the saw. On a shelf in the shed, he noticed a small flashlight and snatched it up, wondering if it still worked. He turned it on, and a steady beam of light cut through the gathering dusk. Good.

He raced along the narrow short-cut path with the saw catching awkwardly at the bushes. As he ran, he heard the wind sweeping through the trees above him, warning of the coming storm.

At last he reached the edge of the clearing. He searched the dim shadows of the spruce trees but he could see nothing suspicious, and all he could hear was his own hard breathing. Lightly, expectantly, he stepped into the courtyard.

Someone had been here. He stared through the gloom at a pile of slashed vines on the ground. The third pillar stood bare.

He dropped the saw, letting it clatter onto the stones, and ran to the pillar. With the vine off, the long, flat stone on top moved aside easily. The flashlight wavered in his hand as he looked into the pillar. He could see fragments of crumbled stone and dangling spider webs: proof that something had once been in there. Now it was gone.

Slowly he turned away. He felt strangely numb inside, as if his ability to hope, to plan, had been paralyzed. All he could think was that he should take the saw back to the tool shed.

He stumbled across the courtyard to where he had left it, following the beam of his flashlight. A tiny point of fire glinted at him from the ground. He bent closer to see what it was and forgot about the saw. From a crevice between the stones he pried out a pale gem that glowed with blue fire when he held it in the light. Instantly he knew that he had found the missing moonstone from Aunt Jeanne's pin.

His fingers tightened around it, although he felt no joy. He dug out the small pillbox that he always carried in his pocket and dropped the moonstone inside. Aunt Jeanne would be glad to see it, but that wasn't what he had wanted to bring her.

Slowly he trudged back through the darkness, trying to prod his dull brain into action. The moonstone hadn't been in the stones of the courtyard before tonight; it was too bright, too easily seen. So it must have been dropped by someone— the same person who had ransacked the pillar.

Kent. It had to be. But how had he known where to look?

"He must have followed me this afternoon," David muttered to himself. "And I led him right to it."

Gradually he became aware that the wind had risen, and now it was blustering through the woods. Aunt Jeanne had been right about the storm. But his feet would not move any faster. It didn't matter if he got wet. Nothing mattered anymore.

Through the swaying trees he glimpsed a light in the hangar. On the next gust of wind came a girl's shrill cry.

That was Kelly's voice.

David shoved the flashlight into his back pocket and dashed toward the hangar as she cried out again. "No, don't! Come back!"

A shadowy figure ran across the pasture in front of him. Where was Kelly?

She darted out of the hangar. For an instant she clung to his arm, and he could feel her trembling.

"David, you've got to stop him," she gasped.

"Who?"

"It's Bruce. He's high on pot—he's crazy. He's got some weird idea that he's going to take off in Dad's plane. He'll crash it. Hurry!"

David was already sprinting across the rough grass. Over his shoulder he called, "Go get someone—up at the house."

Mr. Jonson's airplane loomed ghostly white on the other side of the pasture. Was Bruce inside it?

The airplane's engine roared to life and David ran faster, praying that he wouldn't be too late.

Lights flicked on at wing tip and tail, followed by the long white beams of the landing lights. With a jerk the plane swung around and began to taxi down the pasture toward him. Perhaps he could still stop it—if Bruce hadn't seen him yet.

He dodged the glare of the landing lights and wondered how to get into the plane. Mr. Jonson had been using it for skydivers, so maybe the door was still off.

As the plane drew near, David raced up along the copilot's side and saw that the door was gone—so was the copilot's seat. With one quick step he vaulted over the low sill.

Bruce's out-flung arm caught him on the jaw, sending his head crashing back against the door frame. He rolled into the rear of the plane and crouched there, dazed by pain.

"Coming for a ride, Davey boy? I thought you were scared of airplanes," Bruce shouted above the thunder of the engine.

David ignored the insult. "You can't take off in this weather," he shouted. "There's a storm coming!"

Bruce leaned back in his seat with a peculiar dreamy smile. "I can fly this bird anywhere, anytime. And especially now."

Wind whipped past the small plane, rocking it dangerously. "Hey, you're stoned!" David shouted. "You're in no condition to fly this plane. You'll kill yourself."

"So, who cares?"

"God cares and so does your sister," David shouted back.

"Don't talk to me about her and God," Bruce growled. His face slid into a sly grin. "Saw you down at the river today. Sure had some fun with our slingshots."

He burst into laughter and jammed in the throttle at the same time. The plane rushed across the stubbled pasture, lurching from side to side.

Too fast. He's going too fast! David thought. As they hurtled past the hangar he glimpsed the trees bending before the wind, and a chill shot through him. Bruce was taking off in the wrong direction.

"Watch out!" he shouted. "You're taking off downwind."

Bruce grunted and swerved the airplane. A fierce gust of wind caught it, lifting one wing.

"Don't let it go over!" yelled David. He slid across the floor, clawing for a handhold as the shuddering plane slanted onto one side. While it teetered in the wind, he threw his weight to the upward side and it dropped slowly back to the ground.

He hauled himself upright, fighting to keep his balance in the swaying cockpit. How could he stop this crazy kid before he flipped the plane over?

He leaned toward the instrument panel, searching for the mixture control knob—the one knob he knew would stop the engine.

Suddenly he felt Bruce's hand on his shoulder, shoving brutally hard. He was falling—sliding backward through the open doorway. His feet dropped into nothing. Quickly he grabbed for the door frame and tried to find the landing gear with his feet. But the gear was bouncing as it pounded over the turf. He couldn't keep a foot on it. In another minute he'd fall under those wheels.

He fought to steady himself, and his hands began to slip on the metal door frame. The floundering plane bucked and plunged as if it were trying to fling him off. He gritted his teeth, determined to hang on.

Again the wind snatched at a wing tip. The plane tilted for a sickening moment, then fell back with a jolt that jarred one of David's hands loose. But he had seen the red knob he was looking for, and Bruce was preoccupied now, struggling to control the plane.

He braced his feet against the bumping gear and lunged for the instrument panel.

Pull it now! He ducked under Bruce's swinging arm, yanked the knob back, and wedged his body hard against the seat. With one last snarl, the engine died.

The airplane slowed, veering off to the left. To David's surprise, Bruce shook his head helplessly and sagged back against the seat, allowing the plane to roll to a stop.

Headlights glared outside the cockpit. Bruce frowned at the instrument panel but did not move. Cautiously David leaned across him to take the key from the ignition.

The pilot's door was jerked open by Mr. Jonson. Behind him stood Grandfather. At the sight of their worried faces, Bruce hunched down in his seat, but all his father said was, "Come on, Bruce, time to go home." Bruce allowed himself to be helped from the airplane, and David slid out wearily after him.

As soon as Bruce's feet touched the ground, he pulled away. "No, wait," he mumbled. "I've got to meet Kent. I told him I'd get it for him."

David stepped closer, suddenly alert.

"You're not meeting Kent anywhere," Mr. Jonson said sternly. "He just got picked up by the police at the airport. You'd better not be in on this stealing he's been doing."

Bruce blinked at his father as if he were just waking up. "What are you talking about? I didn't steal anything. I was just going to show it to him." He reached under the pilot's seat and pulled out a small cloth-covered bundle.

Mr. Jonson made an impatient motion while Bruce fumbled with it, but David could not tear his gaze away. Navy blue cloth, dusted with chalky stone fragments. . . . It had to be the coat he'd seen in the pillar.

Bruce let the coat drop on the ground as he cradled a dark wooden box in his hands. "I knew it was in here!" he said triumphantly.

The mahogany box was cracked at the corners, and its surface was dull and spotted with age. Below a tarnished silver plate hung a small lock, badly bent.

Bruce fingered the lock, frowning. "It's been opened." Slowly he lifted the lid. In the red velvet lining of the gun case nestled an old-fashioned powder flask and a bullet mold, but nothing else.

David drew a sharp breath. There were two empty compartments where the silver pistols should have been.

Bruce scowled. "That Kent double-crossed me," he muttered. "I wondered why those vines were so loose. He told me he'd pay me—" Abruptly he stopped talking and, tossing the gun case onto the pilot's seat, he turned away. With sagging shoulders Mr. Jonson led his son toward the car. David stared after them.

Suddenly Kelly stood beside him, her face like a pale flower in the darkness. "I told Dad what you said about Kent and the airport, and he talked to the police." She gave him a heart-warming smile. "Thanks for stopping Bruce. I knew you could do it. And thanks for the verse—I'm claiming it for Bruce too. See you later." She ran to join her father and brother in the car.

Now he was alone with his grandfather. David turned and handed him the key to the airplane, jittery with expectation. What would Grandfather say about the gun case?

But the old man's face was an expressionless mask. In a quiet voice he remarked, "You probably saved Bruce's life tonight. How did you get him to change his mind?"

"I didn't," David answered shortly. "I remembered about the mixture control knob, and I pulled it. Bruce was really spaced-out." All at once he felt enormously tired: saddened by what he had seen in Bruce and bewildered by his grandfather's cold composure.

He picked up Aunt Jeanne's raincoat and gently rewrapped the gun case. How could Grandfather act as if it weren't even here, as if he'd never seen it before?

His grandfather motioned toward the airplane. "Climb in. With this bad weather coming on, we'd better take Bob's plane over closer to the hangar."

While David settled himself on the floor beside the pilot's seat, his grandfather went on talking. "I didn't realize that Bruce was into drugs until just recently." He gave David a quick glance. "That business about sanding the airplane— he was blaming you for something he did, wasn't he?"

"Yes, he must have been high that day," David answered. "What's going to happen to Bruce now?"

"That's what his father came to talk to me about tonight. He's been worried about Bruce and was trying to think of some way to get him away from Kent. There's a good aviation school in Pittsburgh where his aunt and uncle live, so he'll probably send him there."

His grandfather started the airplane, and David clutched miserably at the empty gun case as they taxied over to the hangar. Maybe things would have turned out differently if he had found the pistols first. But Kent had moved too fast.

Remembering how he had found the lost moonstone in the courtyard, David tried to picture what had taken place. As soon as he left the pillar to get the saw, Kent must have sneaked up, cut the vines, and unwrapped the gun case. That's when the moonstone would have fallen out of the raincoat. Probably, after Kent had removed the pistols, he'd rewrapped the box and put it back in the pillar for Bruce to find. Then what?

The pistols were small, but they would make too much of a bulge in Kent's pocket. He must have done something with them in a hurry, planning to get them later.

"Why don't you see whether Bob's tie-down ropes are there in the back?" Grandfather's voice broke into David's thoughts. They had reached the hangar.

He scrambled into the rear of the airplane and found the flashlight he had dropped, but no ropes.

"Well, we can put the plane into the hangar," Grandfather said, and David waited for him to get out of the airplane.

But his grandfather was staring fixedly at the cloth-wrapped gun case, as if he could no longer ignore its presence. David stared at it too, not daring to speak. What was Grandfather thinking?

There was a long silence in the cockpit. Off to the north, lightning flickered over dark masses of swollen clouds. Thunder rumbled. The wind howled around the corners of the hangar, and David felt the little plane sway uneasily.

He stole a look at his grandfather's face and saw that it was twisted with anguish. So he did care, after all.

"David," the old man whispered. "So many years." He brushed an unsteady hand across his face, and David knew that he was talking to the other David, his father, whom he had wronged so long ago.

David felt a confusing mixture of affection and pity for his grandfather. If only the hurt of all those years could be healed!

Finally his grandfather stirred. He stumbled from the cockpit, and David helped him push the plane inside.

As they walked out of the hangar, David stopped. The pistols were still missing. He couldn't give up on them yet.

"Grandfather," he said hurriedly, "I left the saw by the summerhouse. I'm going to run back and get it."

The old man nodded, his face haggard, and David thrust the gun case into his hands. "Go on ahead—I'll be right there." His grandfather shuffled off toward the house with hunched shoulders, as if he carried a great burden instead of an empty gun case.

David turned purposefully into the somber woods. He had to look around the stone house again. Just one more time.

Chapter Eighteen
In Control

He hurried through the storm-tossed trees along the river and into the small clearing. Beside the heap of torn vines, he stopped. Carefully he surveyed the courtyard, trying to think clearly in spite of the anxious thumping of his heart. Where could Kent have hidden those pistols? Not out here.

He stepped into the deeper shadows of the summerhouse, shining his flashlight across the bench and then up to the wasps' nests, high on the stone walls.

His light swept back to the stone bench with the pile of dried leaves under it, and he remembered the first time he had stood here. He dropped to his knees and swept the leaves aside with shaking hands.

The small mound of earth dug by the squirrel was still there. Beside it lay the flat stone. He lifted it, slanting his light into the hole below, and saw the dull gleam of tarnished metal.

Slowly he picked up the pistols, brushing the dirt off them one at a time. He held them close, and the silver barrels felt hard and cold—and real. At last.

Glancing back at the hole, he noticed a small brown package half-hidden in the dirt. As he unfolded the paper bag, a woman's gold necklace slid into his hand. Kent must have been using this hole for hiding the jewelry he'd stolen. No wonder he'd thought to put the pistols here. Without the gun case, they had fit very well.

On his way out of the clearing, David picked up the saw. As he trotted down the path, he wondered what would happen now. Had Grandfather changed his mind about Dad? Would he welcome him back?

He was almost all the way to the house when another question chilled his new happiness. What was Dad's reaction going to be, even if Grandfather did admit that he was wrong? Maybe, after all these years, Dad couldn't forgive him. Maybe he wouldn't want to come back, not ever.

No, David cried out in protest. He had found his family at last: Aunt Jeanne and Nannette and Grandfather. He couldn't leave them now, and Grandfather still needed Christ. Besides, there was Kelly; he was just getting to know her.

He caught himself up short. Had he forgotten already that he had a mighty friend? He could trust Him for all of that—even for Grandfather's salvation. *Fear thou not; for I am with thee: be not dismayed; for I am thy God. . . .* The words kept time with his footsteps as he passed the blackened stump, and peace returned.

He left the saw on the back porch and bounded through the door. Hearing Susan's voice, he followed it to the library, where the gun case lay open on the round table. Susan was holding the powder flask, talking about it to Grandfather and Aunt Jeanne, and the bullet mold was still in the case.

Quietly David put the silver pistols in place, each in its red velvet compartment. The delicate tracery of the engraving still showed through a layer of tarnish. They looked beautiful and deadly.

"You found them!" Susan exclaimed.

Aunt Jeanne flushed pink, and she clutched at the raincoat in her lap. "So you did," she cried. "I thought they were lost forever." She leaned forward eagerly. "Where did I put them?"

"In the third stone pillar." He watched recognition dawn on her face.

"Yes . . . your father and I used to leave messages in there for each other. There is a loose stone on the top." She looked past David with unseeing eyes. "That night after the terrible lightning, I saw fire in the hall. And all I could do was run away."

She turned to Grandfather. "I must have been running to hide the pistols, so they would be safe for David. You said you were going to destroy them."

Pain creased the old man's face. "I was wrong." He spoke slowly, as if each word cost him a great deal. "For all these years, I have been wrong. Perhaps God will forgive me, although I may never see my son again."

"But Grandfather," said Susan, "you don't know about our surprise." She flashed a questioning glance at Aunt Jeanne, who nodded for her to continue. "Guess what? Daddy phoned to say that he's in Philadelphia already, earlier than he planned. He wanted us to meet him there. But I talked to him and so did Aunt Jeanne and Nannette, and he's going to come here. Tomorrow!"

She looked anxiously at Grandfather's stern face. "That's good news, isn't it?"

"Yes," he said after a pause. His expression softened. "That is good news. It is time for my son to come home."

If he still wants to, David thought. He shoved a restless hand into his pocket and his fingers touched the pillbox. "Here's something else I found," he said to Aunt Jeanne. "I think it's yours." He rolled the moonstone into her palm, and she stared at the glowing gem.

"Oh, Dave," she said faintly, "it's the other moonstone. Oh, I'm so glad. How did you find it?"

"It was caught between some stones by the summerhouse."

He told them how he had discovered the bundle in the pillar and had left in order to get the saw. "Kent must have been watching me and decided that he didn't want to pay Bruce for finding the pistols. Maybe he hoped that Bruce would get blamed for stealing them. Either way, when he picked up the gun case and unwrapped it, the stone must have dropped out."

"I was wearing the moonstone brooch the night I ran down to the river," Aunt Jeanne said. "One of the stones was loose, and it could have fallen into my raincoat when I took it off to wrap up the pistols." She smiled at David. "This is a happy day."

Susan wriggled with joy. "It sure is! And tomorrow will be even happier, won't it?" She climbed onto Grandfather's lap.

His keen dark eyes met David's questioning gaze.

"Yes, it will," Grandfather answered, as if he were making a promise.

Aunt Jeanne put a hand on David's shoulder. "Susan is so excited that she forgot to tell you something."

"That's right," Susan said hastily. "Daddy gave me a message 'specially for you. He said, 'Tell David to remember that God is in control.' Do you know what he's talking about?"

David's heart lifted with joy. If Dad had said that, then he must have already forgiven Grandfather.

He turned his head to answer, and the moonstone in Aunt Jeanne's hand caught his eye. The gem shimmered like pearly river fog, reminding him of the morning when he too had allowed God to take control. "Yes," he said slowly, "I'm beginning to understand what Dad meant."

He grinned at his little sister. "Things are going to be okay."